# Uncharted

Anna Hackett

Uncharted

Published by Anna Hackett
Copyright 2016 by Anna Hackett
Cover by Melody Simmons of eBookindiecovers
Edits by Tanya Saari

ISBN (eBook): 978-0-9945572-5-4
ISBN (paperback): 978-0-9945572-7-8

# What readers are saying about Anna's Romances

**At Star's End** – One of Library Journal's Best E-Original Romances for 2014

**Return to Dark Earth** – One of Library Journal's Best E-Original Books for 2015 and two-time SFR Galaxy Awards winner

**The Phoenix Adventures** – SFR Galaxy Award Winner for Most Fun New Series and "Why Isn't This a Movie?" Series

**Beneath a Trojan Moon** – SFR Galaxy Award Winner and RWAus Ella Award Winner

**Hell Squad** – Amazon Bestselling Sci-fi Romance Series and SFR Galaxy Award Winner

"Like Indiana Jones meets Star Wars. A treasure hunt with a steamy romance." – SFF Dragon, review of *Among Galactic Ruins*

"Fun, action-packed read that I thoroughly enjoyed. The romance was steamy, there's a whole heap of supporting characters I can't wait to get to know better and there's enough archeology and history to satisfy my inner geek." – Book Gannet Reviews review of *Undiscovered*

"Strap in, enjoy the heat of romance and the daring of this group of space travellers!" – Di, Top 500 Amazon Reviewer, review of *At Star's End*

**Don't miss out!** For updates about new releases, action romance info, free books, and other fun stuff, sign up for my VIP mailing list and get your *free box set* containing three action-packed romances.

Visit here to get started:

www.annahackettbooks.com

# Chapter One

He edged his hand into a narrow crack in the rock face and readjusted his grip.

Callum Ward shifted his weight and then pulled himself up. Sweat dripped down his face and he pulled in a steady breath, enjoying the pleasant burning sensation in his muscles. Climbing—free of ropes and equipment—was a challenge he enjoyed, along with the adrenaline pumping through his body.

He looked up, his body pressed flat against the warm rock. The Rocky Mountains in spring was one of his favorite places to be.

A world away from the dangers and pressures of the SEAL teams.

*Not a SEAL anymore, Ward.*

Cal stayed there for a moment, breathing deeply. He glanced down at the ground, several hundred feet below him. Then he looked up. The top wasn't far away. With intense concentration, he picked out his path.

Then he climbed.

He loved the speed and freedom of free soloing. He was alive. He couldn't ever let himself forget that.

Or the fact that so many of his SEAL buddies were not.

A few feet from the top, a harsh ringing sound made him start. One of his hands slipped, and for a second, he felt his body swing away from the rock.

Quickly, he moved back, jamming his hand into a narrow handhold, scraping his knuckles in the process.

With a curse, his heartbeat hammering in his ears, he slipped his hand into his pocket and yanked out his cell phone. He wedged the device between his ear and shoulder.

"What?"

"Cal, where are you?" His sister's voice came through loud and clear. "Lazing the day away at your cabin?" Darcy's voice soured. "I hope you don't have company, right now. There's no time for all those blondes tripping over themselves to get to you."

Cal rolled his eyes and glanced at the magnificent view of the valley below—a sweep of trees and the breathtaking mountains. In the distance, he heard the throb of helicopter rotors. Some rich somebody getting a quick transfer to Vale or a rescue helicopter.

"No blonde. I'm climbing, D. Kind of at a critical moment here."

"We have a job."

His senses sharpened. "Okay. Well, I need to finish the climb, get back to my truck, then lock up the cabin. I can be back in Denver this evening."

"Too long. I sent Declan to get you."

Cal snorted. "You managed to pry him away from his new fiancée?"

"It took a little convincing." Darcy's voice softened.

Yeah, Cal's big bro had certainly fallen hard for his sexy little archeologist. It was a little too sickly-sweet to see. Cal couldn't imagine foregoing the variety of lovely ladies out there for just one—no matter how beautiful, smart, or sexy she was.

*Live life to the fullest.* That was Cal's motto.

"Look, it'll still take me some time to meet up with Dec—"

"Actually, he's coming to you. He should almost be there."

At that instant, the sound of the helicopter turned to a roar. The helo crested the mountain top above, sending a fine spray of rocks and twigs raining down on Cal. In the clear bubble of the helicopter cockpit, Cal spotted his brother's rugged face.

Cal sighed. Looked like his climb was done. "Yeah. He found me."

"Good. See you soon."

\*\*\*

An hour later, hair damp from a quick shower, Cal entered the offices of Treasure Hunter Security.

The offices were housed in an old flour mill that Dec and Cal had bought and converted. Dec had outfitted the upper level into his living quarters. Downstairs was all open-plan, with lots of concrete and brick, housing the heart of their business. At one end of the large space, computer screens lined the wall, and high-tech computers sat on sleek desks. That was their sister's domain. Darcy loved anything that involved a keyboard. The other corner was dominated by a pool table and an air hockey table. The furious *thwack* of the pucks told him there was a high-stakes game going on.

"Ward," a deep voice called out. "Come and take over for Morgan. Woman is a fiend at this."

Cal grunted at Logan O'Connor and made his way over to the air hockey table. Logan was big, and with a checked shirt, worn jeans, and shaggy hair, he gave off a wild, mountain-man vibe. His opponent, Morgan Kincaid, was about as opposite to that as you could get. She leaned her long body into the table and shot Logan the finger. The tall, sleek, dark-haired woman wasn't just a fiend at air hockey, she was damned good in the field and in a fight.

She looked Cal's way, her dark hair feathered around her strong face. "Cal."

"Morgan." Cal looked around. "Hale and Ronin?"

"In the field." Morgan strode over to the small fridge in the kitchenette tucked in one corner of the space. She grabbed a soda and popped the top. "Both of them are in DC. Guarding some fancy jewel exhibit for the Smithsonian."

Cal took her end of the hockey table and shot the puck at Logan. "You know I'll beat you too."

"No way, Ward. You're dreaming." Logan slammed it back. "You've never beat me yet."

"That's because you cheat," Cal said.

"Cheat? How the hell can you cheat at air hockey?"

Cal lined up his shot and hit the puck. "I don't know, but you do."

Logan slammed the puck back again with a growl. He shook his head, his shaggy hair brushing his shoulders. "Where the hell is Dec?"

"Well, he dropped me off at my place and then came straight here to meet Layne," Cal answered. "My guess is that he's wrapped around his fiancée."

"He's happy."

Cal lifted his head and studied Logan. Logan was his brother's best friend. The two of them had been together on the same SEAL team, and had saved each other's lives more times than they could count.

"Yeah, he is." Cal was damned happy for his brother. Before Dec had met Layne, he'd carried dark shadows from his time in the Navy. Cal knew what those shadows could do to a man. He'd seen too many friends die, people killed, and bad guys get away. Memories stirred, and he shoved them aside. The shadows could kill you, if you let them.

Dec had gotten out, and Cal had followed not long after. It had taken a bullet for Dec to leave, but for Cal, it had just taken losing his best friend.

"He's in love," Logan added. He made it sound like Dec had caught a disease.

On a security job a few months back, Dec had met Dr. Layne Rush. What was supposed to be a simple archeological dig in the Egyptian desert had turned into a wild and dangerous adventure. Layne and Dec had ended up discovering a lost oasis and falling in love. Now Dec smiled all the time, and snuck his fiancée off to their apartment whenever he could.

Love. Cal had never experienced the emotion, and he was fine with that. "Don't worry, O'Connor, I don't think it's infectious."

Logan grunted.

"The love thing isn't for me." Cal leaned his hip against the air hockey table. "There are too many lovely ladies out there to limit myself to just one."

Logan grunted again. "Like that redhead who was wrapped around you at the bar the other night?"

Cal grinned. "She was…enthusiastic."

"What was her name?"

"She didn't tell me. But we had a great time." They'd gone back to her place, and Cal had left before the sun had come up.

Logan raised a brow. "My prediction…someone is going to make you slow down one day, Ward."

"Nah." Cal liked his life just the way it was. He'd had it serious before. Being a SEAL had meant that every situation was a life or death decision. And every decision could be your last. Treasure Hunter Security suited him just fine. He still got to use his skill set, and he was much less likely to end up dead.

He'd made a vow to a dying friend to live enough for both of them.

"You'll take the fall one day." Logan glanced up,

his gold-brown eyes intense in his rugged face. "Like your brother, you'll be a goner."

Cal shot the man the finger. "Screw you, O'Connor. If you want the whole 'love at first sight' thing so badly, you do it."

Something flickered over the man's face, but before Cal could make sense of it, he heard voices behind them, and footsteps echoing on the polished concrete floor.

Dec, Layne and Darcy had arrived. Dec had one arm slung across the shoulders of his fiancée. Cal guessed he was right in his assessment of what the two had been up to. Layne's attractive face was a little flushed, and his brother looked awfully relaxed and satisfied.

Darcy looked her usual polished self, her high heels clicking on the floor. She was wearing dark slacks and a white shirt that tied up around her neck. Her dark hair swung, shiny and sleek, by her jaw. Darcy might be a hacker extraordinaire, but she always liked to look good doing it.

"We have a job." Darcy's blue-gray eyes leveled on Cal. "Cal, you're going to Cambodia."

Cal groaned. "Why are my jobs never in the Caribbean? Or the Seychelles? Cambodia has jungles, which means mosquitoes."

"So pack some repellent," Dec said, amusement in his deep voice.

Darcy ignored them both. She made her way over to her computers. "We've been hired by the Angkor Archeology Project." She picked up her favorite laser pointer/remote and aimed it at the screen.

An aerial picture of Angkor Wat appeared. The sprawling temple complex was impressive, the central structure rising up from a sea of trees and vegetation. The complex was surrounded by a large moat.

Cal had visited Angkor Wat once before. Not on a job, but while on R and R from his SEAL team. It was a fantastic, interesting place to visit. He wouldn't mind another look at it.

"The AAP is a mixed team of archeologists from around the world, and they are focused on studying the ancient Khmer Empire that flourished from the ninth to thirteenth centuries. The team was responsible for lidar scans that were taken of the area a few years back."

"Lidar?" Logan said.

"Light Detection and Ranging," Darcy answered. "It's a sophisticated scanning technology. The lidar device is mounted on a helicopter that flies over an area, shooting the laser. From it, you get high-resolution maps. The AAP started scanning Angkor Wat, and the scans uncovered amazing detail. Completely undocumented features beneath the forest floor."

The images on the screens changed, showing scans crisscrossed with roads, canals, and earthworks.

"Amazing." Layne stepped forward. "I remember this now. It really helped to expand the knowledge on Khmer construction." She tilted her head.

"There was a lot of hype about a 'lost city' they discovered."

Darcy nodded. "Mahendraparvata. The city was never really lost. Everyone knew where it was, buried under the jungle on Phnom Kulen or Mount Kulen. It's a mountain range not too far away from Angkor." Another image flicked up on the screen. It showed a long silhouette of a mountain. "Phnom Kulen is a sacred mountain, and a few temples have been discovered here and there, but what had been found was mainly just rubble in the jungle. No one really knew the true extent of the city. The scans helped reveal the scale of it, connected the dots, and showed the outlines of things buried beneath the surface."

Cal wandered closer. "So what's so special about this city?"

"Mahendraparvata is the place where King Jayavarman II was crowned as the god king back in the ninth century. It is considered the sacred birthplace of the ancient Khmer Empire."

"So, what do the AAP need from us?" Cal asked.

"The team's recent scans of Phnom Kulen have uncovered some interesting structures." Darcy smiled. "They want security for a jungle expedition to a lost temple."

Cal grinned. "Oh, good. Let me just pack my fedora and bullwhip."

Darcy rolled her eyes at him. "They wouldn't give me details related to these new scans. I'm sure they don't want every amateur treasure hunter or history buff invading. They said they'll provide you with everything you need when you get there. They must have good funding because they're paying well."

"Who are the players?" Dec asked.

"The AAP team is currently staying at a hotel in Siem Reap. That's the main city in the area, and the tourist gateway to the Angkor temples. The team is being led by an English archeologist by the name of Dr. Benjamin Oakley." An unflattering shot of a tall man with a head of gray hair appeared. "He's working with a local archeologist named Dr. Sakada Seng." Another photo appeared showing a young Cambodian man. "Oakley has two more archeologists on the team. An Australian, Dr. Gemma Blake, and a Frenchman Dr. Jean-Luc Laurent." Two more photos appeared beside Dr. Oakley's.

Cal whistled.

Darcy rolled her eyes again.

Dr. Blake was a small, curvy blonde with a wide smile. Laurent looked like he was in his forties, with a long, narrow face and sandy hair.

"The final member of the team is their tech guy. He runs the scanning technology. He's an American by the name of Sam Nath." The picture of a younger man with dark hair, copper skin, and a wide, beaming smile appeared.

"Okay." Cal nodded his head. "So I take this group into the jungle to find a lost temple. I've had worse jobs."

"Oh, there's one extra joining the team as well," Darcy added. "Daniela Navarro."

Layne gasped. "Really? I *love* her work."

Cal frowned. "Another archeologist?"

"You don't know who she is?" Layne shook her head and looked at her fiancé. "You've heard of her, right?"

"Photographer," Dec said.

"That's right." Darcy leaned back against the desk. "She's a world-renowned photographer of ancient sites. She travels the globe, taking pictures of ancient temples, pyramids, and statues. Her photos can go for tens of thousands of dollars."

A picture flashed up. It wasn't of a person; it was of the Abu Simbel temples in Southern Egypt. The photographer had taken the shot early in the morning, the sun just touching the giant statues of Ramses the Great. There was a sense of magic in the shot, a hushed stillness.

It made Cal's chest tighten. Made him think of dreams and possibilities.

"I couldn't find a shot of Navarro." Darcy shrugged. "For a photographer, she doesn't seem to take pictures of herself. But I have to say, her work is fabulous."

Cal knew this would be a straightforward job. Get in, get it done, visit Angkor while he was there, and be back to do some more rock climbing before he knew it. "Well, at least I know our friends at Silk Road won't be interested in the rubble of a temple."

Declan scowled. He and Layne had tangled with the dangerous black market antiquities ring in Egypt. The shadowy organization let nothing get in their way in their rush to steal priceless antiquities.

Darcy nodded. "I don't think those mercenary thieves will bother you. This is a solo job, but if you need more help on the ground, let me know. I'll have Logan on standby."

Logan crossed his arms over his chest. "I hate mosquitos more than Cal."

Everyone ignored him. Dec looked at Cal. "You see any sign of Silk Road, you call us."

Cal nodded and looked back at Darcy. "So when do I leave?"

"Now." His sister handed him a stack of documents. "Enjoy your trip."

***

*Click.*

Dani moved her camera, lining up the girl's smiling face in the middle of the shot, and pressed the button. *Click.* Then she zoomed out, taking in the landmark behind the girl as well.

Dani loved Angkor Wat. The City of Temples was full of amazing wonders. She lowered the camera for a second. Here, at the base of one of the towers of the main temple, the harmonious feel of the place really stood out.

The unique temple rose up into the sky, and its beauty wasn't diminished by the tourists swarming around it. She knew it was a representation of Mount Meru—the sacred mountain that was home of the gods.

What she loved was that every nook and cranny of the place offered something different—amazing bas-reliefs, or nature insinuating itself back into the ruins, trees growing through the temples. She didn't even mind the tourists. Watching them taking it all in, the range of emotions skittering over their faces, it all made her smile.

That's what Dani liked capturing the most. Not just the old temples and the sense of history, but the feelings they elicited. That's what made her photographs come alive—all the things people were thinking and feeling written on their faces and caught in their movements.

Damn, she loved her job. She smiled. She was grateful every day that she made a very good living from her photography.

She zoomed in on a couple posing for their camera that they'd perched on a rock. Young lovers, she decided, by the way they touched each other. She snapped them as they pulled exaggerated poses. Then the man pulled the woman in for a kiss. Dani took the shot, capturing that most elusive of things—love. That fleeting, mysterious emotion.

She lowered the camera. She gave them six months. Then one of them would be itching to get out. She shoved the cynical thought away. *For now, she'd focus on the love.*

Dani set off down the steps and worked her way through the crowd of people walking slowly through the temple. She wandered to a quieter part of the site, where the crowds thinned, and she could hear the echo of her footsteps on the ancient stones. Here, she could get some good shots. She turned in a circle. Hmm, *here*, the light was just right. She raised her well-used Canon.

But there were plenty of pretty shots of Angkor Wat out there. What she was looking forward to the most was her chance to photograph the ruins of Mahendraparvata. Of finding lost temples amongst the jungle.

She stopped again. This time, she spotted a woman only a few years younger than herself. She was gorgeous. Blonde hair spilled over tanned shoulders. She wasn't model thin, instead she had curves that Dani suspected would bring a man to his knees. She felt a flash of envy. When you were tall, with slim hips and a flat chest, curves were always a distant dream. The woman was smiling as she took in the temple's carvings.

As Dani snapped a few more shots, a handsome man wandered closer and struck up a conversation with the woman. They talked for a bit. Small talk, Dani imagined. The woman laughed.

Dani frowned, even as she continued clicking. The man had player written all over him. He had the look of a man who knew what he looked like, and knew how to use it. Her brother and father had the same look—same handsome face, same insincere smile.

With an annoyed sigh, Dani moved on.

She kept snapping shots. She zoomed in, and this time spotted a middle-aged woman dressed in a short skirt and a low-cut top. This time, Dani was reminded of her mother. Julia Navarro Simmons Hall was on marriage number four, and had always judged her worth by her looks. And the bank account of her current husband.

Dani turned away, looking for a more interesting subject. She avoided her family as much as she could. She refused to let them intrude on the life she'd made for herself.

She zoomed in on a man walking up the main path toward the temple.

*Wow.* She took a bunch of shots. Handsome, rugged, and sexy. The man had a face made for the camera with enough angles to cast some interesting shadows. Dark hair that was just long enough to fall over his forehead, day-old scruff on his cheeks, and a well-shaped jaw.

Next, she took in the body. He walked with a loose-hipped stride, a man comfortable with himself. He was somewhere over six feet with a muscular physique. A pale-khaki shirt stretched over wide shoulders, and his long legs were tucked into dark-green cargo pants. He didn't look like a man who spent much time in fancy suits or stuffy offices. No, he was well suited to the ruined temple beside him.

She took a few more shots. Suddenly, he glanced her way, a frown on his face.

Dani decided it was time to move on. She focused on a small group walking up the steps of the temple, and decided to head inside.

Inside the enclosure, bright-green grass contrasted with the old stones. The group she'd followed had disappeared, and instead, Dani focused on getting a few up-close shots of the engravings on the wall. Devatas—dancing women in all different poses, elaborate headdresses on their heads. The entire site was a group of enclosures, galleries, and cloisters leading in to the main temple.

She wandered up some steps and into a paved gallery. She paused, taking a deep breath. Here, she could easily imagine the ancient Cambodians walking through on their way to celebrate their gods.

"Hey, stop!"

The young woman's scared voice made Dani frown. She hurried around the corner.

Down a set of steps, she spotted a man playing tug-of-war with a woman's backpack.

The man kept yanking, but the woman held on with grim tenacity.

Suddenly, the man shifted his weight and shoved hard against the woman. She stumbled backward but kept her bag clutched in her hands.

"Hey!" Dani let her camera drop around her neck and hurried down the steps. "Leave her alone."

The man's dark eyes widened. Ignoring Dani, he reached down and gripped the woman's bag again. She cried out and fell onto her hands and knees.

"I said, leave her alone." Dani rushed forward, and slammed a hard kick into the man's side.

He stumbled back with a grunt. He was a couple of inches shorter than Dani's five foot eight, but she didn't dismiss his wiry strength.

When he raised a fist, Dani got mad. She kicked him again and slammed her fist into his belly.

"Stop!"

The deep, masculine voice echoed off the temple walls. Behind her, Dani heard the sound of running feet. The thief's gaze went over her shoulder, and his eyes widened.

He turned and bolted.

Chest heaving, Dani turned. And went still.

Mr. Handsome, rugged, and sexy was sprinting toward her.

# Chapter Two

Dani watched the man leap down the stairs and run two steps past her before stopping. The attacker had disappeared into the temple ruins.

Blue eyes settled on Dani. Something about the look on his face made the hairs on the back of her neck rise. No wonder the bag-snatcher had taken one look and fled.

The man's blue gaze flicked to the young woman getting to her feet. "You both okay?"

The woman nodded and looked at Dani. "Thanks to you. You were amazing."

"Happy to help," Dani said.

The woman pushed her light-brown hair back and patted her backpack. "I've got everything in here. My wallet, passport, camera... I can't thank you enough."

"You should report this," the man said.

The woman gave him a long once-over and smiled. "Unfortunately, I have to meet my tour group in twenty minutes. I'll talk to my guide." She lifted a hand. "Thanks again." The woman hurried off.

"You got in some good hits."

Dani looked up. "Thanks."

Tall, dark, and rugged smiled. "Those were some nice moves."

A flicker of heat in her belly. *God, down, hormones.* "Always pays to know how to kick a man's ass."

The man's brows rose, a gleam in his eyes. "Maybe you've been hanging around with the wrong kind of man."

Dani made a sound and checked to make sure her camera was okay. "Only one kind, in my experience."

"You think I'm going to snatch your backpack? I can assure you, I'm not. I actually work in security."

She watched him shove his hands in his pockets and shoot her a charming smile. Oh yeah, the guy was good-looking. And he knew how to work it.

"I'm not worried about my backpack." She cocked her head. "Why do I get the feeling you've used the 'I work in security' line before?"

"Well, it *is* my line of work..."

"Right."

"People usually find it interesting."

"Mmm-hmm."

"But I can see it isn't really working on you."

"You security guys are observant." She looked at her watch. "Well, look at the time. Unfortunately, I have someplace I need to be."

His face turned serious. "Look, I was impressed with the way you jumped in to help that woman. And the way you brought that guy down." He smiled again. "I'm used to being the one doing the rescuing."

She made an *uh-huh* sound.

"And I have a meeting I need to get to as well, but how about we meet up later? I can buy you a drink...prove to you that all men aren't out to steal your backpack."

The guy was lethal. That smile, that face, the body.

Dani had seen her brother Joshua pull out the same smile, the same charm. God, her father was even more practiced at it.

She was immune to it.

"No, thanks." She lifted her camera and then opened her backpack. She pulled out a different lens from the specially-designed slots in the bag, and then swung the bag back onto her shoulder.

The man frowned. "No?"

Had he never heard the word before? "That's right."

"Why?" His sexy, cajoling drawl was gone.

"Because I don't spend time with men like you."

He tilted his head. "Men like me...?"

"Yes. Ones who are interested in a drink or two, then a quick romp between the sheets. You'll be all charm and sexiness until you spot the next pretty, shiny young thing that comes your way."

"There's nothing wrong with that, as long as everyone's up-front with each other."

"Right. And I'm being up-front." Dani clipped the new lens on the Canon. "You could catch up with the woman we helped. You'd probably have better luck with her."

"Clearly."

The confused, annoyed look on his face caught her attention. It made her want to smile. Instead, she lifted her camera and snapped his photo.

He reached out and grabbed her camera. "It's polite to ask first."

She pulled her camera back toward her. He tugged it back toward him.

Dani tugged again. "I don't really bother with being polite."

"Yeah, I got that."

She pulled a face. "It usually means I miss my shot. If people know I'm taking their photo, they get stiff and awkward."

"I'd prefer if you ask me, first. And believe me, I was already feeling stiff and awkward before you took the picture."

She yanked the camera back.

He shook his head. "Someone did a number on you, didn't they?"

Dani's stomach turned over.

The man gave her another long look. "Life's too short to spend it all twisted up."

Before she could think of a good comeback, the man turned and strode away.

She huffed out a breath. *Right.* Well, she was due back at the hotel to meet the rest of the team.

Time to leave the temples—and the people inside them—behind, and set to work capturing the discovery of a new one.

She didn't stop to take any pictures as she

headed out of the temple complex. Out the front, she jumped into one of the waiting cabs and held on for dear life as her driver tried to break the land-speed record on the way back to the hotel.

When they stopped, Dani shoved a wad of Cambodian riel at her cab driver—who grinned at her wildly—and stepped out of the battered vehicle.

The Heritage Hotel was really beautiful. Nestled amongst tropical walled gardens, the building was a neoclassical design of cream stone with lots of arches. Inside, the rooms were simple, but elegant, with dark wood accents and Cambodian art on the walls. She felt that familiar urge deep inside and lifted her camera.

She snapped a few shots of the hotel façade. While it may not have been the most luxurious hotel in the city, it had a charm and beauty about it. Plus, it was pretty darn comfortable. She'd stayed in a lot of interesting places while she was working—yurts in Mongolia, Bedouin camps in North Africa, even an ice hotel in Finland. The Heritage Hotel was getting no complaints from her.

As she took her shots, she noted a rugged four-wheel-drive parked in front of the hotel. A motorcycle was strapped to a rack at the back of it. Now, *that* was a vehicle made for adventure.

She hurried inside. The meeting with the archeologists was in ten minutes, and she didn't want to be late. Inside, the air was cooler, and she took a second to enjoy it against her skin.

"Did you follow me?"

The deep voice had her glancing up...into

familiar blue eyes.

"No." She frowned. "Did you follow me?"

Tall-rugged-and-knew-it crossed his arms over his chest. "Sorry, sweetheart, I'm staying here. Actually, I'm meeting the team I'm working with in a few minutes."

Security specialist. Her stomach turned over. *Great.* "Not the Angkor Archeological Project."

His gaze sharpened, dropping to her camera then back to her face. "You're Daniela Navarro."

She frowned. "How do you know my name?"

"I know you're the photographer for the AAP. And I'm the new security specialist."

"Oh." That was all Dani could manage.

"I'm Callum Ward. Treasure Hunter Security." He held out a hand. "This is the part where we act politely and you pretend you can work with a 'man like me.'"

"You were just itching to say that, weren't you?"

"Yep."

Dani settled her camera around her neck and held back a wince. Steeling herself, she thrust her hand into his. His palm was large and callused. After a quick shake, he just kept holding her hand.

"Well, Mr. Ward. Welcome to the adventure."

His thumb brushed over her wrist, and the move sent a tingle up her arm. *Strange.* She tried to pull her hand back.

He refused to let it go. "Call me Cal."

She gave her hand a hard tug. "And I'm Dani."

"But Daniela is so much prettier."

"And so much longer. Are you going to let go of my hand?"

He smiled at her. "When I'm ready. I can't place your accent, Dani."

"I was raised mostly in the US. But my father is Portuguese."

"*Fala portuguese?*"

"*Sim.*" Curiosity winged through her. "Your accent is very good."

Cal smiled. And damn if it didn't make that already attractive face more compelling. "I speak five languages, thanks to my previous employment."

She let her gaze drift down his body. "I'm guessing military, or an agent of some description."

His brows winged up. "How the hell would you know that?"

"I take pictures of people for a living. I'm good at reading things about them from what they look like, how they move."

He inclined his head. "Navy SEAL."

Special Forces. He might be a handsome man with a good deal of charm, but it also sounded like he was no superficial player. You didn't make the SEAL teams without a hell of a lot of skill and grit.

"But now, I do private security." A faint smile on his lips. "Although I know that doesn't impress you much."

She blinked, connecting the dots. "Ward. I had the pleasure of meeting your mother once."

Cal's smile widened. "Oh. I bet that was an experience."

It had been. Persephone Ward was a tiny woman with a huge personality. Dani eyed Cal, unable to believe the small, energetic treasure hunter with the big reputation had given birth to this hard, dangerous, sexy man. "It was on an expedition in Brazil. She was amazing."

Cal's face softened. "Mom has that effect on people."

"Mr. Ward?"

The crisp British accent made Dani smile. "Here comes Dr. Oakley."

They both turned and saw the archeologist hurrying into the hotel lobby.

He offered Cal a polite smile and held out his hand. "I see you've met Dani."

Dani watched the men shake hands. They couldn't have been more different. The older, reserved man of study, and the younger, edgier man of action. She wanted to take a picture of them, but ignored the itch.

"Welcome to Cambodia," Dr. Oakley said. "Actually, Dani only arrived yesterday as well, and it's a pleasure to have you joining our team. With help from both of you, we're going to do something wonderful."

Dani managed a smile. Now she was going to be trapped in a jungle with sexy Callum Ward. Lord help her.

Oblivious to her struggle, Dr. Oakley waved them across the lobby. "The others are meeting us in the bar. Shall we go?"

Cal turned to Dani. "Looks like I get to buy you a drink, after all."

***

Cal sat down on one of the comfy chairs in the hotel bar, a bottle of cold beer nestled in his hand.

Dr. Oakley settled in the chair beside him. "The others should be here soon."

Cal nodded and took a sip of his drink. As he did, he tracked Dani Navarro wandering around the room, camera in hand.

She was one prickly, annoying woman. Shame it was in such an attractive package. She was on the tall side for a woman, slim, small breasts and long legs. He'd always had a thing for long legs. He let his gaze trace down them. Even in simple cargo pants, it was far too easy to imagine them wrapped around his hips.

God, and that face and hair. Her face was damn near perfect, with lots of interesting angles. At Angkor, he'd noticed she had eyes that were different colors—one green and one brown. And it was hard to miss the hair. Long, black curls that she kept pulled back in a tail. It made him wonder what they would look like loose, particularly with his hands tangled in them.

Plus, she smelled good. She looked all businesslike in her sensible clothes made for trekking around a temple, and holding her camera. But the woman smelled like sin. Her perfume was something spicy that made him think of harems and hot nights.

The snarky words she'd thrown at him at the temple rang in his ears.

She wasn't wrong. He liked to have fun with a woman. But he never lied, and tried not to hurt anyone. She didn't have to act like he was a damned serial killer.

"Here they are."

Dr. Oakley's voice dragged Cal's attention off Dani. Four others were settling into the chairs around them.

"Cal, I'd like to introduce Drs. Blake, Laurent, and Seng." Oakley nodded at each. "And the final member of our team, Sam Nath."

Cal studied the newcomers, recognizing them all from their pictures.

"Hello. I'm Gemma." Dr. Gemma Blake gave him a wide smile and leaned in close to him. Her Australian accent added to the attractive package she made. "You're a welcome addition to our little gang."

He smiled at her. "Cal Ward."

It took him about one second to note the annoyed look on Sam's face. It seemed their tech guru had the hots for Dr. Blake.

"Jean-Luc Laurent."

Cal shook hands with the French archeologist, and then with the Cambodian.

"Sakada." The local archeologist's English was near-perfect. "A pleasure to meet you."

"Happy to be working with you all." Cal leaned forward. "So, Dr. Oakley, why don't you tell me about this expedition?"

The man nodded. "Well, you know about the scans…"

Cal sipped his beer. "Right, the lost city that wasn't really lost."

Oakley laughed. "Right. The media sensationalized it a bit. But what the original scanning project allowed us to do was reveal the true extent of Angkor and Mahendraparvata on Mount Kulen." The archeologist pulled out a tablet and set it on the small table in front of them. He swiped the display and scanning maps filled the screen.

"Mahendraparvata is where the first Khmer king was crowned," Gemma said. "It's really a fascinating and important part of Cambodian history. And the city has just been lying buried in the jungle all this time."

Cal listened as the archeologists peppered him with information about the site. He leaned back in his chair, and while he absorbed the information, he watched Dani wandering near the windows. She moved with the liquid kind of grace that he admired.

But there was something…lonely about her. Like she wasn't connected to all the people and places she was studying. She was an observer, separate from the action.

Gemma bumped her arm against him. "Would you like to hear about the coronation?"

*Focus on the job, Ward.* "Sure."

It was Dr. Oakley who answered. "It begins with

the Hindu practice of devaraja—the cult of the god king. A ceremony was used to crown a king as a deity, a god king. Jayavarman II was the first to introduce the practice to this area. Prior to that, the country was all small warlord states, but he joined them all together."

"A Brahman was brought in to conduct the devaraja ceremony," Gemma said. "He used a sacred stone called a linga as part of the ceremony. It contains the essence of the Hindu god Shiva and conveys that power to the king, so he becomes the god king or the king of kings."

"Linga?" Cal tapped a finger against his beer bottle. "I've done some work in India before, and I've seen linga there."

Gemma smiled and leaned closer. "That's right. A linga is a phallic-shaped stone that represents the energy and potential of Shiva."

Cal got the impression that Dr. Blake was quite fond of linga.

"This linga used by Jayavarman was said to be a magical stone," Sakada said.

Dr. Oakley leaned forward, his face eager. "We've been able to excavate some parts of Mahendraparvata, at least, what's easily accessible. We uncovered mention of another temple located deeper in the jungles of Phnom Kulen. The Temple of the Sacred Linga."

"I seem to recall linga shrines were fairly common," Cal said.

"This one is unique," Dr. Oakley said. "A temple dedicated to the linga used to crown Jayavarman."

"There are several mentions of this temple in different sources," Jean-Luc added. "Based on this, we got funding to carry out more lidar scans on an area of the mountain that we hadn't looked at before." He looked beside him. "Sam?"

The younger man grabbed the tablet and turned it around. He tapped the screen and then swiveled it so Cal could see the images. "These are the new scans. It's an uncharted area of Phnom Kulen. It's the thickest jungle on the mountain, and even the locals don't go there."

Cal studied the map, noting out of the corner of his eye that Dani had moved closer and was looking over his shoulder. On the screen, he could see the outlines of *something* beneath the jungle.

"The temple was likely built in the distinctive quincunx formation, representing the sacred Mount Meru," Sakada added. "Four towers at the corners and a fifth in the center."

Then Cal saw it, in amongst the lines on the map— a vague square outline of a temple.

He looked up at them all. "Okay, so we need to get to here?"

"That's it." Dr. Oakley nodded. "The Temple of the Sacred Linga."

"Sam, can you send me a copy to my email?" Cal asked, handing him a business card.

The man nodded.

"We might even find the magical linga in the temple," Gemma said. "I wouldn't be surprised. There are already clues that lingas were particularly sacred on Phnom Kulen. Have you heard of the River of a Thousand Lingas?"

Cal looked up and caught Dani's eye roll. "I can't say I have."

Gemma's smile widened. "It's a popular tourist destination on Phnom Kulen. A stretch of the river there has thousands of linga images carved into the rocky bottom of the river."

"And other sculptures as well," Sakada added. "Quincunx designs, as well as images of gods and goddesses, nagas."

"Nagas?" Cal asked.

"Serpent deities," Sakada answered. "Cambodian legend says they were a reptilian race who helped create the Cambodian people."

Gemma's eyes gleamed. "I know the Temple of the Sacred Linga is there, just waiting for us to find it."

Cal couldn't fault the archeologist for her enthusiasm for her work. "Okay, I'll make plans to get us there and ensure we have all the supplies we need." Thoughts ran through his mind as he planned out the trip in his head. He'd need to get Darcy to send him information on Phnom Kulen and the mountain's jungles. "We'll need camping gear as well."

"When do you think we can leave?" Dr. Oakley asked. "We're eager to get started."

"Tomorrow morning."

Oakley's brows rose to his hairline. "So soon?"

Cal smiled. "We have a very good team at Treasure Hunter Security. Let me get to work, and I'll have everything arranged."

"Very good," Dr. Oakley said. "Now I know why you came so highly recommended. We've arranged a dinner tonight to celebrate the beginning of our expedition."

"I'll need to get my work finished first, but dinner sounds great."

When Oakley lifted his glass of wine, Cal lifted his beer and they clinked them together.

"To a good expedition," Dr. Oakley said.

The rest of the team traded clinks. Cal stood and moved over to where Dani stood alone by the bar, sipping what looked like a gin and tonic. He lifted his bottle.

She let her glass touch his. "In their eagerness, they forgot to mention that Phnom Kulen was used by the Khmer Rouge in the seventies, as their final stronghold. Parts of the mountain are riddled with old landmines."

"Nothing I can't handle."

"Well, to a successful trip, then," she said.

"These days, I'm just happy when no one is shooting at me."

"I'll be shooting you," she muttered. Then the corners of her lips quirked into a smile. "With my camera."

"A camera I can handle." He leaned his elbows on the bar. "But it always pays to be prepared for the worst."

# Chapter Three

Dani zoomed in on Cal's face and hit the shutter button. She'd call this one *smart toughness*.

Behind her, she heard the tinkle of Gemma's laugh, and cutlery hitting plates. The team had shared a meal in a private dining room off the hotel's restaurant. The others were still picking at the delicious local foods, but Cal had eaten quickly and gone back to work.

He was currently standing at a long table pushed up against one wall, looking for all the world like he was planning for war.

A map covered the table, and he was leaning over it, his sleeves rolled up and showing off his muscular arms. He was jotting down notes on a paper pad, and a tough-looking tablet was propped up against some books. Dani snapped another shot. She'd already pegged him as tough. Treasure Hunter Security had a reputation for it.

But as he frowned, tapping the pen against the map, she realized she hadn't expected the sharp intelligence she saw on his face.

"You sure we'll be ready to leave tomorrow?" she asked.

He looked up. "That's the plan. You want to get out there, right?"

"Oh, yes." *There*. That look on his face. She had to capture it. She lifted her camera again.

He shot her an irritated look.

"You have a face the camera likes. A rugged sort of handsome."

"You think I'm handsome?" A smile flirted around his lips.

"I'm stating that in a purely factual way. And I'm pretty sure you know exactly what you look like."

"How's the planning going?" A voice interrupted their conversation.

They both turned as Dr. Oakley appeared.

"Great," Cal said. "I've got our route mapped out, local guides organized, and I'm just waiting for a call from my office in Denver to confirm the last details. But we'll be ready to go in the morning."

"Wonderful."

The excited look on Dr. Oakley's face had Dani turning her camera his way. She zoomed in on his face and clicked.

Then she swiveled to Cal and took a shot of the answering smile on his face. He scowled at her again.

Suddenly, the tablet on the table flared to life. A woman with dark hair in a sleek bob and blue-gray eyes appeared. "Hi, Cal."

"D, my love. How's Denver?"

"Fabulous. You'd know if you spent any time here."

"You keep sending me on jobs."

The woman was beautiful. Black hair, pretty face, a crisp shirt that matched the color of her eyes.

The woman's smile sent her from beautiful to stunning. "I'll schedule you a vacation. You can take me up to that little cabin of yours in the mountain for a weekend."

"It's a date," Cal replied.

Dani frowned. He was making a date? Right now?

The woman's face turned serious. "Okay, ready?"

"Hit me," Cal said.

"I've organized another four-wheel-drive vehicle for you. It's stocked. I've arranged everything you need from food to basic camping supplies. You saw my email about the best route to Phnom Kulen, and the names of the local guides from the villages."

"Got it. Made a few tweaks."

"You always do. You'll meet the guides at a site called Srah Damrei. It's also called Elephant Pond."

"Excellent. You're a marvel."

"Of course."

The others wandered over from the dining table. Cal nodded at them. "Everyone, this is Darcy. She's our tech whiz and organization expert back at Treasure Hunter Security headquarters."

The group called out greetings.

"Hi. Okay, at Srah Damrei, the local guides will be bringing motorbikes. The tracks into the temple site are too narrow and overgrown for cars."

There were a few groans from the team.

Dani watched as Cal shot questions at Darcy, and the woman deftly fired back answers. Clearly, she was organized and well prepared. Smart and beautiful. Dani didn't like her.

"D, amazing as always. What would I do without you?"

She shot him a sour look that didn't lose any of its impact across the computer. "And you are a charmer. Remember it doesn't work on me."

"Love you, D."

The easy camaraderie between the two, and those words Cal had just said, hit Dani in the gut. She decided not to hang around to hear any more. She backed away. The words "love you" were cheap when she was growing up. Her parents had tossed them around like confetti. Apparently, Callum Ward did, as well.

She heard Gemma call out. "Let's have one last drink to celebrate."

Dani slipped through the large French doors, and into the lobby. She felt a familiar, driving need to take more pictures. From the first moment one of her nannies had given her a camera, she'd felt the instant spark to capture the world around her.

She made her way past the reception desk, and headed out the front door. Outside, she pulled in a deep breath of fresh night air. Without thinking too much about it, she turned and walked down the street toward the main part of town. Soon, the quiet street gave way to the hustle and bustle of

Siem Reap's busy center. The crowds thickened.

Dani lifted her camera. She spotted a family—tourists—walking together. All of them were sunburned, but happy, the parents sharing a funny moment with their teenage kids. There were plenty of locals, some sitting together, some working, others out on the town. Everywhere, there was noise, lights, life.

It was so different from the reverence of the ancient temples just a few kilometers away. There, Dani had captured the quieter, tranquil moments. There was so much depth to be caught in the stillness.

Here, it was all about the movement.

She moved deeper into the crowds, into the heart of the bustle. No one paid her much attention, which was how she liked it. But, as a group of laughing women passed her, she wondered how she could feel so alone in the middle of all this.

A couple passed, arms twined, smiling up at each other. Why was she still thinking about love? And the fact that, while her parents had said the words to her many times, they'd never meant them. They'd never shown her any kind of love.

Jeez, she was getting miserable over old news. She set her shoulders back and shrugged off the stupid thoughts. She moved along the street, taking pictures of the buildings jammed together, and ahead, the bright colors of the night market. Neon lights glowed, and the bright-colored stalls offered all kinds of trinkets.

Before she reached the market, she stopped at

the entrance to an alley. She aimed her camera. Down here was the darker, danker, dirtier underbelly of the city. It wasn't pretty, and it wasn't fun, but it was still part of life.

Her photography gave her everything she needed. She didn't need meaningless words. She didn't need anything but the camera in her hands. Right here, she had the power to experience and capture love, hate, joy, despair...any emotion, all without ever letting it affect her. Without ever letting it break her into tiny painful pieces.

Someone bumped into her.

Figuring it was a tourist not watching where they were going, she turned with a smile.

The second shove was harder, and sent her sprawling to the ground in the alley. As her hands and knees scraped across the dirty concrete, she felt the sting. Her camera dangled from the strap around her neck, bumping her chin.

The next thing she realized, someone was grabbing at her camera, yanking hard. The strap dug painfully into her neck.

A mugging. *No way*. She pulled back and tried to scramble away. No one was taking her camera.

She looked up. The man attacking her had a scarf covering the majority of his face, so she couldn't tell what he looked like. He strode toward her and lunged at her again.

With a cry, Dani dodged his grasp, and pushed to her feet. Getting her balance, she raised her hands and turned to defend herself.

The man swung out, trying to grab her camera

again. Dani let instinct take over. She'd taken multiple self-defense courses. She kicked, aiming for between the man's legs. But he was quick and moved at the last minute. Still, she got a good kick into his thigh and she heard him grunt.

But he recovered quickly, dark eyes settling on her.

He moved fast, grabbed her shoulders, and spun her. Her back hit the brick wall and all the air rushed out of her. He raised a large fist and Dani fought to get free.

*Dammit.* This was going to hurt.

Then, suddenly, he was pulled backward.

Dani fell to her knees, confused. For a second, she thought the shadows had grabbed him. Then, she saw the silhouette of a tall, muscled man in the darkness. He had a good grip on her attacker.

The would-be thief was slammed hard against the wall of the building. Then her rescuer smashed a hard punch into the man's face.

The men moved again, spinning around. The attacker let loose with a series of wild, desperate punches, but the taller man retaliated with powerful, restrained blows.

They scuffled a bit more, and then suddenly her attacker broke free and sprinted out of the alley.

Dani got one foot under herself as her rescuer turned to face her.

Cal Ward's blue gaze met hers.

***

Cal reached down and helped Dani to her feet. "You okay?"

She looked pissed. There wasn't a single flicker of fear in her face. A smile of reluctant admiration tugged at his lips.

"I'm fine." She dusted off her trousers and then lifted her camera and checked it. "This camera's been around the world, and it's not the first time someone's tried to snatch it. Probably won't be the last."

Cal's instincts were screaming at him. He hadn't seen much under the man's black scarf, but the man had been focused and experienced. He hadn't seemed like a random thief after a quick buck.

"I'm not even that attached to this particular camera," Dani continued. "I'm not the kind of photographer that spends a fortune on a camera and treats it like a treasure. I replace the body every year." She shrugged. "I didn't want to lose the photos I'd taken."

"He could have hurt you."

Her chin lifted and her hands tightened on the Canon. "This is mine and no one is getting their hands on it." Then she winced. "Ow."

Cal gripped her wrist and turned over her palm. When he saw the raw, angry scrapes, fury punched through him. He looked down and saw her knees hadn't fared much better—her trousers were torn. "Come on. We better get you cleaned up. I can't imagine what could be in this alley."

She grimaced. "Good point."

Cal held her arm and pulled her back out onto

the busy street. As the crowd nudged them together, he pulled her closer into his body. He needed to contact Darcy and have her check things out. He didn't like that Dani had been attacked…something felt off.

If Silk Road was sniffing around his job, it wasn't good news. He frowned to himself. This had to be random. Silk Road wouldn't be interested in this ruined temple. Rocks wouldn't get them much on the black market.

When he spotted a tuk-tuk, he waved it down. "I have a first aid kit back at the hotel."

They settled into the open-air carriage attached to a motorbike. Cal gave the driver the address and they zoomed off.

"Why were you down here?" she asked

He shrugged. He'd seen her slip out of the planning meeting…and hell, he wasn't even sure why he'd followed her. "I saw you leave. I'm in charge of your safety now."

She stared at him for a second. "I've been looking after myself for a very long time, Ward."

"Well, for the next little while, you won't be."

The tuk-tuk ducked and weaved through the traffic, and it knocked them into each other. She stared at him a bit longer, before she turned her head to look out the side of the vehicle.

She looked cool, a little tough, but the way she gripped her camera hinted that beneath that barbed exterior was something a little warmer and softer.

She flipped her camera over, and the screen on

the back flickered to life. She started shuffling through her shots. Cal leaned over and watched as she studied them, making a few noises here and there. When it came to her work, he saw the way she came alive.

One image of Angkor Wat made his breath hitch. Damn, she was good. There was another of the busy street they'd just left behind. He shook his head. Someone who could make a busy, crowded, dirty street look magical had a hell of a lot of talent.

Suddenly, he saw one of himself. He was leaning over the map back at the hotel, his palms pressed to the table. Hell, somehow she'd made him look like a general planning out a battle strategy. She'd captured the crease between his brow, the intensity in his eyes. He looked up at her face. She somehow turned the ordinary into something else in a single image.

The tuk-tuk weaved again and they bumped shoulders. She pulled back from him instantly.

"You don't like me," he said.

She shrugged. "I don't know you. But you remind me of my brother."

"Ouch."

A faint smile. "You don't look like him." She tilted the camera toward him. It was a shot of him smiling at Darcy on the tablet. Dani flicked again and it showed another of him with Gemma pressed up against his side. "Joshua is slim, stylish, and has very soft hands." She looked down at Cal's hands before glancing at his well-worn cargo pants.

"Joshua wouldn't be caught dead in anything so unstylish. He likes designer." Her gaze moved up to Cal's face. Some emotion crossed her face before she looked away. "Joshua is a playboy. Follows in my father's footsteps."

"Oh?"

Dani's smile turned brittle. "My father is onto wife number five. She's younger than I am. I think Joshua is on fiancée...number three. I've lost track."

"I can assure you, I've never been married or engaged," Cal said.

"But you love women. All women. You turn on the charm."

"Yeah, I do." He stared at her, suddenly feeling a flash of insight. "Darcy is my sister."

Dani's hands stilled on her camera. "Oh."

"I like to enjoy life, Dani." He gestured to her camera. "Not hide from it behind other things. There are too many shitty moments, so it pays to find some good ones when you can."

The tuk-tuk stopped. Cal leaned forward and paid the driver. "Come on, let's get those wounds cleaned."

Dani stepped out. "I can take care of it myself—"

Cal clamped his hand around her arm. "I didn't say you couldn't. Doesn't change the fact that I'm going to clean your injuries. Last thing I need is you risking infection while we're in the jungle."

She sighed and followed him. They stopped by his room and Cal took a second to grab his field first aid kit, then he followed her down the hall to her room.

She unlocked her door and, once inside, turned on the lights. She instantly moved to an open case on the table and set her camera carefully inside it.

The room was similar to his. Glossy wood floors, a simple four-poster bed made of dark wood with white, gauzy hangings. There was framed Cambodian art on the walls and above her bed was an excellent photograph of Angkor at sunset. A cream ceramic tub sat out in the open by the window. For one glorious second, he imagined her in there—only slim legs and shoulders above the bubbles.

She walked into the adjoining bathroom and ran the water in the sink. She started washing her hands, and winced visibly.

He walked in, crowding her against the sink. He felt her stiffen. Yeah, she wasn't as unaffected by him as she liked to think. He wet a washcloth and then shut off the water.

"Sit on the bed."

She shot him an annoyed glance, but did as he directed, and dropped onto the bed. Cal bent one knee and knelt in front of her, opening the first aid kit. He grabbed one of her hands, turning it over. He tried not to wince when he saw the damage to her palm. It wasn't bad, but it had to sting. He started wiping at her abraded skin.

Cal had guessed a man was to blame for Dani's protective shell. And he knew he'd guessed right, just not in the way he'd thought. "You aren't close to your family?"

She shrugged. "They're busy with their vacations, parties, designer clothes, cheating on their current partners, affairs, sex. It's all so...frivolous."

Cal moved to her other hand. She had long, narrow fingers, and kept her nails clipped short. "You think sex is frivolous?"

"Yes. God, I grew up watching my parents act like teenagers." She pulled a face. "I caught my mother with the pool boy when I was eight. My father with my mother's best friend when I was twelve. My brother with my underage friend when I was fourteen. My brother decided on the 'if you can't beat 'em, join 'em approach.'" Dani shrugged. "I don't have time for sex. It's a lot of time and effort for not much payoff."

Cal stilled and looked up. "Sex doesn't have to be frivolous. And if you do it right, the payoff can be very good." He slid his hand along her wrist, feeling the tick of her pulse. "Hands are done. I need to see to your knees now. You'll have to take your trousers off."

He expected flushed cheeks and hesitation. He should have known she'd surprise him.

She stood up and worked the buttons on her trousers free. The material fell to the floor at her feet. "I don't think I'll take any advice on un-frivolous sex from you."

She sat back on the bed. She had well-formed legs; no doubt her travels kept her in good shape. Her shirt pooled in her lap, and damned if Cal's fingers didn't itch to shift it out of the way.

He slid his hand along her calf. When he reached her knee, he grabbed the cloth and set to work cleaning.

"It's about enjoying yourself. Taking your time to see what you and your partner like." He moved his other hand behind her knee, touching her smooth skin. Her spicy, sexy perfume was taunting him. The woman smelled like sin. "I bet it's much like getting the perfect photograph. You have to take your time, learn what works and what doesn't. And for each person you shoot, it's different." Gently, he finished cleaning her wound. "Each person is an individual, and they find pleasure in different things."

"Oh." Her voice sounded a little breathy. "And here I had you pegged as a 'wham bam, thank you ma'am' kind of guy."

"You just keep making these assumptions about me." Then he grinned. "But hard, fast and sweaty...that can be fun too." He saw her chest was rising and falling a little more quickly now.

"You are not what you appear at first glance, are you?"

"None of us are. I thought you'd know that better than anyone. I think through your lens you see things people don't want you to see."

She was watching him with a mixture of curiosity, desire, and wariness. Damn, Cal really wanted to kiss her. Wanted to push her back on that big bed and see what made her cry out his name.

But then there was a burst of laughter from the hall outside, and it broke the moment. Cal leaned back and stood.

Dani Navarro wasn't fun and easy. She was prickly and intense…things he avoided.

He cleared his throat. "We have an early start tomorrow. You should get some rest."

She nodded. "Thanks for playing doctor."

A naughty comment played on his lips but he swallowed it back. "I'll leave some antiseptic cream and bandages here for you. Put them on in the morning."

"Sure."

Hell. Why did she have to look so damned delicious sitting there with her bare legs? And that sinful perfume…it was all he could smell.

"Sleep well."

"You too."

He closed her door behind him. Yeah, he'd sleep…after a cold shower.

*** 

Darcy Ward stared at her brother's image on the computer screen. "Cal, you're sure? A black scarf over his face?"

"I was fighting with him, D. Up close and personal. It was a black scarf, and the guy was definitely after Dani's camera. Roughed her up trying to get it."

*Damn.* This was not good. Darcy tapped on her keyboard. "It's standard Silk Road MO. Their goons always wear a black mask or scarf."

Her brother uttered a curse. "It could still be random. One black scarf isn't exactly damning."

"You want to take that risk?"

Her brother sighed. "No."

"And Dani's okay?"

"Just scrapes and bruises. I helped her clean them up." He smiled. "She fought back like a trooper."

Darcy paused, studying Cal's handsome face. There was something in his voice when he spoke about the photographer. "You like her."

Cal made a sound. "The woman is prickly as hell. She has a messed up family…she's more likely to smack a man than kiss him." A scowl. "Or take his photo without permission."

Hmm, this sounded interesting. Darcy leaned back in her desk chair. Cal was used to women falling all over themselves to get to him.

Still, right now, she needed to focus on finding information on Silk Road.

"Cal, have the archeologists mentioned any valuable artifacts associated with this lost temple of theirs?"

"Sure. The temple is dedicated to a magic stone shaped like a penis."

Darcy's lips twitched. "Hmm. Well, maybe Silk Road is branching out."

Cal shot her an answering smile. "You find out anything, you call me."

"I will." She glanced at the clock and calculated the time difference. "You should get some sleep. Be careful heading into the jungle tomorrow."

Cal tossed her a lazy salute and the screen blinked off.

Darcy got to work trying to see if there was anything linking Silk Road to Cambodia. While Cal was heading to bed, her day was just getting started. She leaned over her computer and got busy. The morning melted into afternoon. After a quick lunch with Declan and Layne, Darcy headed back to work.

God, Dec and Layne were perfect for each other. Seeing her oldest brother so happy was amazing. Now, if she could just get Cal to slow down. He was always climbing this or racing that. He claimed he was living life to the fullest, but it had only really kicked in since his best friend Marty had died.

His friend's death had scarred Cal. And now the man never stopped—he was addicted to adrenaline and speed.

A chime sounded. Her nails clicked on the keys as she pulled up the info on one of the screens on the wall.

It was a blurry image of a tall redhead. The woman's face was obscured but apparently it was one of the few confirmed photos of a woman named Raven. No last name on file.

She was suspected of having links to Silk Road. And she'd landed in Cambodia two weeks ago.

Darcy stroked her chin. She didn't like this at all. She ran some more searches. Who was this Raven woman? What "links" to Silk Road did she have? And why was she in Cambodia?

Darcy needed answers.

Suddenly, a warning flashed up on the screen: *Restricted Access.*

*What?* Frowning, she used her less-than-legal hacking skills to get past the restrictions. The computer chimed again and a modulated voice said, "Warning. Someone is hacking your system. Warning."

All the screens on the wall went blank.

*No way.* Heart pounding in her chest, she hunched over her keyboard, fingers flying. Darcy's love affair with computers and coding had started as a shy preteen. She was good. Damn good.

And no one hacked her system.

She punched in commands, swearing under her breath.

A single screen flicked on. "Ms. Ward, do you speak like that around your mother?"

Staring at the screen, shock sucked her breath away. "Special Agent Burke. My mother taught me the curse words." Fury punched through Darcy. "How dare you hack my system! This is an invasion of privacy—"

"Cool it." His impassive face was one step too far past rugged to be handsome. But with laser-sharp green eyes, five-o'clock shadow on his jaw, and short, brown hair, there was no denying Agent Burke made an impact.

Damn him.

Although Darcy was usually too busy noticing his condescending, arrogant attitude to worry about what he looked like.

"You were accessing information sensitive to a case. You could have tipped them off and jeopardized our investigation—"

"I don't give a crap about the FBI's investigation." Burke headed up the Art Crime Division, specializing in art and antiquities theft. "My brother is in the field and if Silk Road is going after him, I'm going to help him any way I can."

Agent Burke frowned. "Declan?"

"No, Callum." She wavered, wondering how much to tell him. He might annoy the hell out of her with his holier-than-thou manner, but sometimes he helped them. When he wasn't busy getting in their way. "He's working for the Angkor Archeology Project in Cambodia. They're in the jungle, heading to explore the ruins of an undiscovered temple on Phnom Kulen."

Burke's face sharpened. "Cambodia."

"I just said that," she said with a huff.

He muttered under his breath, looking torn.

She leaned forward. "You know something?"

"Darcy, a group of Silk Road mercenaries have just landed in Cambodia."

Darcy froze. "To meet a woman called Raven?"

His gaze narrowed. "That's right. She's in charge. She's former Russian Intelligence and she's ruthless. You need to warn Cal to stay away."

"What are they after?"

"I don't know exactly. All I know is that they are hunting a valuable artifact in the jungle."

That wasn't very specific. "Well, Cal isn't after any treasure. This has to be a coincidence."

"I don't believe in coincidences," Burke said.

Nor did Darcy. "I'll warn Cal." And organize some backup for him. She steeled herself. "Thank you." Okay, that sounded normal. Not stilted at all.

Shockingly, a faint smile crossed Agent Burke's serious face. "Two words I never thought to hear from you."

She screwed up her nose. "You could accept it graciously instead of being rude."

"Ah, there's that sharp tongue of yours."

"I'm going now." She waved a dismissive hand at him. "Tell your team of FBI geek hackers that they're good. I'm impressed that they got into my system."

Burke's smile widened. "No geeks. I did it myself."

She blinked. "What?"

"I've been practicing."

The screen went black and he was gone. A second later, all the screens flicked back on, her system returning to normal. Darcy stared at the screen for a moment, easily picturing his face.

Then she shook her head. She needed to pull this information together and contact Cal.

Silk Road was close and she needed to warn him.

# Chapter Four

After breakfast, Dani walked outside into the early morning sunshine. The rest of the team was already out there, packing the vehicles. There was a feeling of excitement shimmering in the air.

She instantly spotted Cal, and that made her pause.

Last night, after he'd left her, she'd lay in bed a long time, unable to sleep. She'd been thinking of him and the things he'd said. The way he'd looked in that alley—intense and lethal. The way his callused hands had felt on her skin, the way he'd tended her injuries, the heat in his eyes as he'd watched her.

Okay, that wasn't all she'd thought about. She'd wondered—in graphic detail—what he looked like with his clothes off. She pressed her hand to her forehead and rubbed. It was just the photographer in her. She was itching to photograph him. That was it.

She sighed. She sucked at lying to herself.

"Okay, people, we need to get moving." Cal patted the hood of his four-wheel-drive. "It'll take us a couple of hours to get to Phnom Kulen. Sam will drive this vehicle, and most of you can go with him. My vehicle's filled with the extra supplies we need, so I only have room for one passenger."

"Oh, I'll ride with you, Cal," Gemma said.

Dani hitched her backpack up on her shoulder, her jaw tight, and started down the steps.

Sam pushed forward. "Gemma, I wanted to discuss some of the scans with you on the drive."

The female archeologist's smile faded and she huffed out a breath. "Oh...fine." She winked at Cal. "Sorry. Next time, I'm all yours."

By the time Dani reached the cars, the rest of the team had filled Sam's four-wheel-drive. That left her with Cal.

She opened the passenger-side door.

Cal grinned at her from across the car. "Sleep well?"

"Like a baby."

"I've always gotten the impression babies cried a lot and woke up frequently."

She arched her brow. "How many babies have you been around?"

She saw a slightly panicked look cross his face. "Ah...not many."

Dani slid into the car. As she settled her camera in her lap and dumped her bag on the floor, Cal climbed into the driver's seat. She glanced over her shoulder and studied the neatly stacked boxes and bags.

Cal started the vehicle. "Let's get this show on the road."

They traveled slowly through the just-waking Siem Reap. Every now and then, Dani snapped a shot of something that took her interest, but the light wasn't bright enough yet for her to be able to get anything good. Soon, they were out of the city, surrounded by fields. The sun rose fully, casting a golden light on clusters of coconut trees, spindly wooden huts, and sodden rice paddies.

Cal's hands gripped the steering wheel with ease, driving with a lazy confidence. They were strong hands, decorated with a few nicks and scars. Dani had always appreciated hands that showed a life well lived.

"That's Phnom Kulen in the distance," Cal said.

Dani saw the long, blue shadow of the mountain range in the distance. "So is this what most of your jobs are like? Heading off on an adventure, trekking through jungles and deserts?"

He turned his head. "Mostly. We do security for museum exhibits as well, so sometimes I get jobs in civilization. But my skills are most suited to trips like these."

"Your secret Navy SEAL skills?"

A flash of white teeth. "Yep. Can't tell you what they are, though, or then I'd have to kill you. They're classified."

She rolled her eyes. "That cliché has been done to death. Do the ladies still fall for that one?"

"Contrary to your belief, I don't spend all my time trolling bars to pick up women. When I'm not on a mission, I'm usually in Denver. I like rock-climbing, skydiving, any sort of extreme sport."

"So you're an adrenaline junkie as well."

He grinned. "I like to go fast. And if I meet a

woman who's looking to enjoy some time together, I take her up on that. I'm upfront about the fact that I'm not looking for a long-term relationship. That's honesty, Dani. Would you prefer I lie to a woman?"

Dani shifted in her seat. "I think that's just an excuse commitment-phobic men use to avoid entanglements."

"I have entanglements. I have a family who is always in my business. I work with them, so they're really hard to avoid sometimes."

Dani tilted her head. She heard the warmth and affection in his voice. "You're close to your family?"

"Yes. My brother and sister are co-owners of Treasure Hunter Security with me, so I see them almost every day. We're all close with our parents as well."

Dani couldn't imagine it. "Must be nice."

He snorted. "Oh, sure, especially when they are giving me hell for something. Personal boundaries mean nothing to my mother or my sister. They are both more than happy to let me know what they think, all of the time."

Dani wondered what it would have been like to have a mother who didn't mostly forget about her. "Still sounds nice. Your mom is certainly…unique."

He laughed. "That's one word for her. Luckily, my dad is the calm, patient type. They balance each other out."

"He's a professor, right?"

Cal nodded. "Dr. Oliver Ward. Professor of History at the University of Denver. They've been married for almost forty years, have raised three kids, are still dedicated to their careers, and are crazy in love."

Dani couldn't quite believe it. "But that's not something you want?"

"One day, maybe." He glanced her way again. "So, you're on the road a lot?"

She nodded. "I love traveling. All the different countries, cultures, people. I'm happiest with my camera in my hand and a beautiful temple in front of me."

"Doesn't it get lonely sometimes?"

"How can I be lonely with so many people around me?" She looked out the window. She wasn't going to admit to those times, lost in a crowd, when it seemed like no one even saw her.

"It's easy to get lost in the crowd." Fingers brushed at Dani's ear and cheek.

She shot him a cool look. "Keep your hands to yourself, Ward."

He held his hand up. "I bet you use that cool, vaguely-pissed-off look to get the guys to back off. I kind of like it."

She rolled her eyes.

"Saw that." He grinned at her, then took a deep breath. "Damn, I like the way you smell, too. Spicy, sexy, lush…it's so at odds with your thorny exterior. Gives me ideas."

Dani pressed her head back against the headrest and vowed to change her perfume. "All right…let's just get it out there. We're attracted to each other."

"Dani, attracted is a really mild word for it."

She turned to look at him, and wished he didn't

have to look so sexy with that scruff on his face, his blue eyes glinting. "It would be a mistake to act on it. I'm here to take photos. You're here to do your security thing. We don't have time for this."

"I kind of like making mistakes. Especially when they feel so good."

She sighed. The guy was incorrigible.

"In these situations, my friend Marty used to always say to just sit back and enjoy the ride."

"Where's Marty now?"

Cal's smile dissolved, his hands flexing on the wheel.

She felt the painful throb of grief in the close confines of the vehicle. She lowered her voice. "Cal—?"

"Dead. He's dead."

Since his tone warned her he didn't want to talk about it, she lifted her camera and started to take some photos of the scenery.

As Phnom Kulen got closer, the roads got narrower and bumpier. They left the fields behind, and the road became a dirt track lined by lush, green grass. As they headed up the mountain, the jungle closed in around them, and the number of cracks and pot-holes in the path increased.

After an hour, Cal pulled off the road onto another. The trees grew tall here, vines hanging down from them, filling the area with dappled light. A flat space opened up ahead, and Cal pulled the vehicle to a stop. "We're here."

"Where is 'here', exactly?"

"Srah Damrei, also called Elephant Pond. A srah

or a baray was a Khmer construction. A rectangular reservoir of water."

"I don't see any water."

"Not anymore. But look." He pointed through the windshield.

It was then Dani noticed them. The giant carvings of an elephant and several lions, rising up from the jungle floor.

"Wow." She gripped her camera, and with her other hand, pushed open her door.

Cal grabbed her arm. "Don't wander off too far. This is a tourist spot, so you probably don't have to worry about landmines...but there are other dangers."

She tossed him a salute. "You got it, General."

"It was Commander." He grabbed her wrist and moved her hand until her fingers almost touched her brow. "This is how you do a proper salute."

He leaned across the car, their bodies close. He took up far too much of the space. His callused fingers brushed her skin, causing her heart to skip a beat.

He went still. "Dani...you don't want to look at me that way."

She huffed out a breath. "Dammit, I can't seem to help but look at you."

His eyes flashed, his hand sliding down to cup her jaw.

Air whistled between her teeth. "Yesterday, I could blame my attraction on adrenaline."

"You always tell the truth?"

"Yes. I hate lies and pretenses."

His fingers tightened on her "I won't lie to you, Dani." His mouth moved closer, hovering over hers. "Now, let's make a really big mistake."

She tried to fight it, but desire, need, and want were making her mindless. "Dammit to hell." She cupped the back of his head and yanked his mouth to hers.

*God.* It was exactly how she'd imagined it, what she wanted. Fierce, edgy and hungry.

His firm lips moved over hers, his tongue sliding in to command her mouth. Blood was roaring through her head, desire a hot, sharp burn through her belly. She threw everything into the kiss, her hand sliding into his hair.

He groaned, his hands flexing on her skin. Then he pulled back. "Jesus."

They stared at each other for a second, and it was then the other Jeep pulled in beside them.

"Hell of a mistake, Navarro," Cal said.

"Yeah."

He touched her hair. "I really want to see this loose, tangled in my hands as I fuck you."

She let out a shaky breath. "The others are getting out of the car."

Cal still didn't release her. They stayed there, staring into each other's eyes.

It was only the roar of engines that made him let her go and sit back. Dani glanced through the window and saw motorbikes tearing into the parking lot.

Dani climbed out and watched as Cal went to shake hands with the local guides. Damn the man was so potent. So dangerous.

She looked around until her gaze snagged on the nearby stone elephant. It was near life-sized, covered in moss. He was gorgeous in the dappled light. She lifted her camera and got to work.

Soon, her emotions evened out, along with her pulse. She felt steady again, even in the soupy heat of the jungle. She took several shots of the elephant, and then the lions nearby.

They looked amazing, rising out of the green of the jungle. What other wonders were waiting for them on this trip?

She sensed someone beside her and spotted Cal. He was watching her, hands on his hips, a faint smile on his mouth.

"You go somewhere else when you're taking photos."

She nodded. "Especially when I have such great subjects." She gently touched the cool stone of the elephant. "He's gorgeous."

"Bikes are almost all loaded with our supplies. We're ready to head off."

As the others moved closer, Cal turned to address the group. "Okay, let me introduce our guides." He went through the introductions, Sakada doing most of the translation. A few of the guides spoke some broken English. "We're going to split everyone up," Cal added. "Each of you will be on the back of a bike with a guide."

"Thank the lord," Gemma said. "I didn't want to be riding one of these things myself."

Dani studied the simple motorbikes and then

saw Cal pulling his own bike off the back of the Jeep. She glanced at the assembled group. "There are only five guides." And the rest of the team was climbing onto the bikes with them.

Cal smiled at her. "You're with me."

\*\*\*

Cal climbed onto the motorbike and started the engine. He glanced over his shoulder at Dani.

The look on her face as she stared at the bike almost made him smile. "I promise I'm a good rider."

With a resigned sigh, she slipped the strap of her camera around her neck and climbed on between the supplies and him. "Why am I not surprised?" She looked around. "What am I supposed to hold on to?"

"Me."

He heard her mumble something under her breath, and then her arms wrapped around his waist. She shifted, getting comfortable, and Cal had to admit, having Dani Navarro pressed up against him really wasn't a bad thing. "Ready?"

"As I'll ever be."

Cal checked on the others, and saw the guides had loaded the last of the gear. He signaled the lead guide, a man named Arn. Then Cal revved the engine and they set off.

At first, the track they followed was well-used, winding through the jungle trees. Golden light filtered down between the trees above.

They whizzed along, and soon the track turned bumpier. They crossed rickety wooden bridges, and a few times, the jungle gave way to small farms. One moment, a bright burst of sunlight would blind them, then they'd be swallowed again by the jungle.

As Dani adjusted to the bike, Cal felt her relaxing behind him. Soon, she was only holding on to him with one hand, the other lifting her camera to try and take pictures. He shook his head. No surprise there.

As they crossed through another small farm, he spotted a small mound of dirt ahead. Deciding she was comfortable enough, he aimed for it. "Hold on," he shouted.

Both her arms wrapped tight around him. He shot over the mound, and they jumped into the air, landing with a bounce.

Behind him, Dani laughed. Her mouth brushed his ear. "Again."

Soon, the track got wilder and more overgrown. This was a place few people ventured. Cal signaled to Arn for them to take a break.

The bikes pulled to a stop. Cal set his boots on the ground. "We'll stop here for a short rest. Grab a drink and a snack. Stretch your legs."

Dr. Oakley climbed off his bike and pressed his hands into his lower back. He arched backward with a groan. "I might be getting too old for this."

"You want to discover the temple, right?" Jean-Luc nudged the other man with a smile.

Oakley nodded. "Yes. Yes."

Cal saw that same eager, hungry look in all the archeologists' eyes that he saw on every expedition he went on. The ones that worked in the field were adventurers at heart.

In moments, the others were fishing in their backpacks, pulling out water bottles and granola bars. The local guides sat down, eating their own food.

Dani, of course, was taking photographs.

He wandered closer to her. "Take the chance to grab a snack."

"Yes, Commander." This time she gave him a perfect salute.

"You're a quick learner."

She sat down under a tree, opening her pack. "And don't you forget it."

On a fallen branch nearby, Cal spotted a flash of movement. Something green.

His instincts kicked in. He dived forward, tackling Dani to the ground. A second later he was on his feet, pulling her with him.

"What the hell?" she gasped.

He spun her, keeping her in the confines of his arms. "Look."

When she saw the bright-green snake, she gasped.

It slithered off the branch it had been resting on, its bright-yellow eyes looking in their direction. Then it disappeared into the jungle undergrowth.

"Greentree pit viper," Cal said. "Highly venomous. Pit vipers are responsible for a hell of a lot of deaths in Cambodia. You need to be more careful out here."

Dani raised a shaky hand and pushed her hair back off her face. "You got it. Snakes are not my favorite thing." A look flowed over her face. "Wish I'd gotten a picture of it, though."

Cal rolled his eyes. He'd never met a woman like Dani Navarro before.

Soon, everyone was back on the bikes, bouncing along the jungle track. Slowly, the tracks got narrower and more overgrown, causing them to travel much more slowly. Vines slapped at their faces, and in a few places, Cal and the guides had to stop to cut a way through with machetes.

Cal kept consulting Sam's map to the temple site. They were heading in the right direction.

Moments later, Cal heard shouts and saw Dr. Oakley waving wildly in his direction. Cal pulled the bike to a stop.

Oakley had already slid off, and was hurrying over to what looked like a pile of rocks in the trees.

That's when Cal realized it was ruins.

"Check for snakes first," he called out.

The team crouched around, studying the moss-covered rubble. Cal decided it had probably been the base of a tower or statue. The archeologists took notes and conferred with each other. Dani circled them, taking pictures.

"There are ruins like this all over the mountain," Dr. Oakley said. "Remnants of Mahendraparvata—unmarked and never explored." He stroked a hand over one of the stones. "It's hard to tell what this once was…now it belongs to the jungle."

Sam held up his tablet, the map showing on the screen. "Well, the Temple of the Sacred Linga is one piece of history we're going to claim back."

Gemma bumped a shoulder against the man. "Okay, Indiana Jones."

"Let's keep moving," Cal said.

They climbed on the bikes again. Cal waited until Dani's arm was wrapped around him tight and they moved on.

She pressed against him, leaning forward so her mouth was pressed to his ear. "I'm getting used to the bike. When do I get to drive?"

"Never," he called back.

"It's a man thing, right?"

"No, it's a Cal thing. I'm pretty happy sitting here with your thighs wrapped around me."

He heard her snort.

But he'd told her the truth. Feeling her pressed up against him, her hands resting on his abdomen...he liked it a lot.

The track got harder to travel. The trees were thick and the vines thicker. Soon the guides pulled to a stop. They had a spirited conversation in Cambodian.

Cal looked at Sakada. The archeologist was frowning. He shot a few questions at the guide before shaking his head. "They say they won't go any farther. The tracks are very overgrown, hard even for the motorbikes." The man's frown deepened. "But on top of that, they say it is a cursed area beyond here. There are bad spirits, and no one should go in."

*Damn.* Cal had known they'd have to trek part of the way but he'd hoped to get closer to the temple location. And he'd been on too many expeditions to argue with people over their beliefs and traditions. If the guides didn't want to go in, no way he'd force them.

This would have to be good enough. "Thank them, Sakada."

There was another round of conversation.

Sakada gave a nod. "They will go to the nearest village. Two of them are from there. They will keep the bikes ready for our return."

"Okay, people," Cal called out. "From here, we hike in on foot." From the side of his bike, he pulled out his machete and grabbed his backpack. "Everyone will need to take their packs and some of the gear. I also suggest you make good use of your mosquito repellant. We only have a few hours of daylight left. So let's get moving."

The guides left with a roar of engines. Cal strapped some of the lightweight tents to his pack and pulled it onto his back. He checked to see the others were all ready and then started slashing a path through the jungle. He heard the click of a camera and glanced behind him. Dani was crouched, the camera blocking most of her face.

"Ask," he said

She lowered the camera and looked up at him. "May I take your picture, please?" Her tone was saccharine-sweet.

He lowered his voice. "Only if I can take yours later." The image of her naked and spread across one of the four-poster beds back at the hotel flashed through his head.

Her face changed. "No."

He detected something in her tone. "Why not?"

She shrugged and stood. "Photographs in my family were all about being lined up wearing our Sunday best. I inevitably got my clothes dirty or messed up my hair. My mother was never happy." Dani lifted the camera "I prefer to be on *this* side of the camera."

Cal moved closer, so only she could hear him. "I could get a good shot of you. And so you won't worry about dirty clothes, you could be naked on silk sheets. I think that would suit you."

Her lips parted, then she shook her head. "Jungle to cut down, Ward. You'd better focus on that."

With a laugh, he did. Cal had used a machete too many times to count, and got into his usual rhythm, hacking away the vines and undergrowth to make a path for them. Jean-Luc and Sakada proved pretty good with the machetes as well. While they couldn't move as fast as they had on the bikes, they were making good progress, moving deeper into the uncharted jungle. Every now and then, they passed piles of rubble or weathered statues. Hints of the remnants of the lost city resting beneath the vegetation.

"You enjoy this." Dani had caught up to him again.

Cal paused and swiped his arm across his sweaty forehead. "Beats a war zone."

"The SEAL teams...it was rough?"

"War is." His gut turned over. "I lost some good friends."

"Like your friend Marty?"

His gut went hard now. "Yeah. Like Marty."

"I'm sorry." She paused. "You said your brother was a SEAL, as well?"

"Yeah. Dec took a bullet and got out."

"I guess providing security for archeologists, even on remote expeditions, is safer than what you did before."

Cal grunted. "You'd think. Actually, Dec took a bullet a few months back on a job. He almost died."

Dani blinked. "I thought chasing artifacts would be less dangerous than fighting bad guys."

"Usually. Some jobs are downright boring. But Dec was on a job in Egypt and tangled with some antiquities thieves."

He saw Dani's eyes widen. "The Zerzura discovery? That was your brother?"

"Yep."

"Oh, I would give my first born child to photograph there. A lost, underground oasis in the desert...I can only imagine the images I could capture there." Her mouth slid into a frown. "They aren't letting anyone in there, yet. I've tried."

"It is pretty amazing."

She pulled to a stop. "You've been there?"

God, her face. "I went in with our team to rescue Dec and Layne, the archeologist he was with."

To be honest, Cal hadn't really paid that much attention to the ancient city carved into the rock walls of the underground oasis. He'd been too busy saving Dec's life. His brother had been bleeding out from a bullet wound.

Cal channeled extra energy into hacking away at the vines in front of them. Just the memory of his brother, bloody and dying, reminded Cal of the friend he hadn't been able to save.

Suddenly his blade hit rock with a clang.

Beside him, Dani gasped. He reached out and pushed aside the vines.

Staring back at them, was a stone statue.

The seven-headed snake rose up like a cobra. The statue was taller than Cal, and badly weathered.

"Beautiful," Dr. Oakley said. He was a little out of breath, sweat beading on his face. "A naga. The Cambodian people believe they came from the union of a Brahman and the daughter of a naga king."

Cal pushed back more vines. "There's another statue behind it."

Dani's camera clicked as she took a shot. Cal frowned. He couldn't tell what the hell the other statue was. Some sort of monster.

Behind them, the other archeologists moved closer.

"Oh, my God," Gemma breathed. "It looks like a makara."

Sakada nodded. "Yes, definitely a makara."

Cal decided it looked like an elephant with the tail of a fish. "Which is what?"

Sakada looked at him. "A sea monster. Usually

half terrestrial animal, like an elephant or crocodile, with the tail of a fish or seal."

Dr. Oakley stepped forward, an excited light in his eyes. "The makara was considered a guardian of the gateway or threshold." He smiled. "We're getting close to the temple."

# Chapter Five

Dani stopped and slipped a new memory card into her camera. She was getting so many great shots. She loved the jungle. She loved the feeling of teeming life all around her. It almost made up for the sticky humidity and the mosquitos.

But she could tell the light was slowly disappearing. They'd have to stop soon.

She slapped a branch away from her face. Having to hike put you up close and personal with the jungle and its wildlife. Although, she had to admit she liked being on the bike as well. Okay, maybe she just liked being pressed up against Cal. Feeling the warmth of his back against her, feeling the hard ridges of his stomach under her hand.

She shook her head. She was supposed to be focused on her work, not talking herself into a wild case of lust.

But as she watched him swinging the machete, sweat dripping down his temples and soaking the neckline of his shirt, she had to admit that she was starting to like him.

With a deep breath, Dani turned her attention to the rest of the group. Dr. Oakley was looking tired but determined. Sakada looked like he was having the time of his life. Jean-Luc and Gemma were a bit wilted but still going strong. Sam looked like he'd prefer to be somewhere else.

Then Gemma cried out with excitement, and the other archeologists pushed forward.

Dani swiveled, and saw the tower rising up into the trees.

It reminded her strongly of the towers at Angkor, but this one had a tree growing over it. She took a few shots of it, cursing the dying light.

Jean-Luc crouched at the base of it to scratch away some of the dead plant life. Dr. Oakley circled it, talking with Gemma and Sakada. Dani took pictures of them as a group, then individually. Their feelings were clearly written all over their faces. She liked seeing such very different people, joined together by a common passion.

Cal stood watching, the tip of his machete pressed to the ground. "Get what you need because we can't stay long. We're losing the light."

Dr. Oakley nodded. "Thanks, Cal. We just need to take some photos and document this." He smiled and the weariness disappeared. "There are references to the linga temple here."

Cal nodded. "I'll take a look around. No one wander off too far."

Dani lost herself in her work—the quiet whirr of her camera, the muted light of the jungle. She blocked out the voices of the archeologists, not really paying any attention to them. She framed the ruined tower and thought of the long-ago people who'd built it, worshiped at it.

She moved away from the others, circling around the back of the ruin, stepping over tangled tree roots. Then she heard a noise and frowned. At first, the noise didn't register, and she rounded the worn stones.

Dani's eyebrows snapped up to her hairline. Gemma and Sam were pressed up against the stone wall of the tower. The tech guy had his hands clamped on the archeologist's ass, and Gemma had her hands down Sam's loosened pants.

"Ah…sorry." Dani took a backward step.

Sam jerked back like he'd been electrocuted. His eyes were just a little wide, and he swiped his hand across his mouth. "Um… I'd better get back to work. Dr. O wanted me to finish getting photos of the engravings."

Gemma looked unconcerned, and took her time tucking her shirt back into her trousers. She shot Dani a smile. "I like younger men. They're so…energetic and enthusiastic." Her smile widened. "They trip over themselves to do everything I ask."

Dani made what she hoped was an appropriate noise.

"Of course, I wouldn't mind a crack at something as sexy and dangerous as Cal. A man like that gives a woman ideas."

An ugly feeling slashed through Dani's gut, her hands clamping around her camera.

Gemma redid the tie in her hair. "Those older, more experienced tough guys bring something very different to the table." Now Gemma winked. "Or should I say bed… Or even a ruined temple."

Dani couldn't help but snort out a laugh.

"But I get when guys aren't that interested in me." Gemma walked toward Dani. "And Callum Ward is not taken by my charms." She stopped, shoulder-to-shoulder with Dani. "You need to grab that hard body, girl, explore every inch of it, then ride him into exhaustion."

Dani's breath hitched. "I'm not really into meaningless sex."

Gemma's eyebrows rose. "You need a ring?"

"No. But some sort of commitment…"

Gemma shook her head. "Dani, there is nothing wrong with a strong, sexual woman taking what makes her feel good. If you want my advice—"

"Not really, but I get the feeling you're going to give it to me anyway."

Gemma grinned. "Yep. Enjoy the right now. Especially if it looks like Callum Ward."

The archeologist walked away and Dani let out a long breath. She tilted her camera and flipped through some shots until she spotted one of Cal. He was standing tall, sexy stubble on his face, sweat dampening his shirt, and the machete in hand. All that fierce concentration…

With a shake of her head, Dani gingerly stepped over broken stones that had fallen from the tower. She needed to get a few more shots of the ruin and the team before they moved on.

She'd only taken a few steps, when someone slammed a hand over her mouth. Panic and adrenaline pumped through her. She jabbed an elbow back and heard a man grunt.

She exploded into action. She elbowed him again, and twisted. Kicking him was too awkward, so she focused on breaking his hold. She shoved her arms down hard.

He cursed in what sounded like Russian, and she got a flash of dark hair and dark eyes. And a scarf pulled over his face.

He made another sound—an annoyed one—then clamped his arms harder around her, trapping her arms against her sides. He started dragging her back toward the trees.

Dani kept fighting. She slammed her head back into his face.

With a yowl, he let her go. She was already turning to punch him, when Cal stormed past her.

Cal's blow hit the man in the side of the head. He struck back, but Cal was ready, blocking him and delivering another vicious hit to the back of the man's neck. Her attacker grunted, then spun and charged at Cal.

The man's arms wrapped around Cal's middle and both men went flying. They knocked into Dani, and she fell forward on her hands and knees, rotting leaves sticking to her fingers.

She scrambled away, her camera bumping against her chest. She spun and saw Cal and her attacker wrestling on the ground.

Neither of them made much noise, and it was clear both of them knew how to fight. Cal landed a brutal chop against the man's arm. The man retaliated, striking out with a fist, but Cal moved, quick as a snake, and dodged. Dani tried to see the attacker's face, but the scarf hid most of it. He was a little shorter than Cal, but stocky and muscular.

Cal kicked the man in the gut, the man stumbling backward. Cal moved in, and with two more vicious hits, the man fell to his knees and then slumped to the ground, unconscious.

The fight was over.

Cal pulled out some zip ties and secured the man. "Okay?" Cal crouched beside Dani and touched her face.

She nodded. "I'm fine. Thank you."

"Looked like you were doing okay on your own." He grabbed her hand and helped her to her feet. He looked back at the tower. "We need to get to the others. You need to stay quiet. I think there are more of them."

Her stomach cramped. More of them? "Who the hell are they?"

Cal's face hardened. "I have my suspicions."

She followed behind Cal as they circled the ruin. She wondered how the hell he could move so quietly. His steps were silent, while with every one of hers she heard the crunch of twigs and leaves under her boots.

Suddenly, he stopped, and lifted his hand. She froze right behind him, her hand pressed against the cool rock of the tower. The sound of conversation carried to her ears.

"What do you want?" It was Dr. Oakley's strained voice.

She heard the sound of someone being hit. Dr.

Oakley let out a cry, and Dani heard Gemma's sob.

"I'm okay." Dr. Oakley's voice was more subdued now.

Cal crouched and peered around the tower. Dani followed his movements.

She stifled a gasp. Their team members were all on their knees and four men were standing nearby, all wearing black scarves over their faces. One man was emptying out everyone's backpacks and their other bags.

"Stay here." Cal's voice was a quiet whisper. He pulled his gun from his holster.

Dani swallowed. "I can help you."

"No." His voice brooked no argument. "I need you to stay here. That's what will help me. I don't need to worry about you." His blue eyes flashed.

"Four against one, Cal. That isn't good odds."

"I've had worse."

"I can help."

"No."

"Yes."

"Dammit," he bit out. "You are so stubborn."

"I won't do anything stupid," she promised.

"Here." He grabbed the machete off his belt and handed it to her. "Anyone comes your way, you swing it at them."

Dani hadn't realized how heavy the damn thing was. She nodded.

Then she watched as Cal's face changed. The sexy, easygoing charm melted away. It left a hard, serious face that shouted "don't fuck with me."

Cal suddenly cupped the back of her head and

yanked her forward. The kiss was quick and hard. "Stay safe." Then he turned and stalked toward the group.

Dani followed behind, staying back and out of his way. If he needed help, she'd be ready.

Cal didn't rush and he didn't look concerned. Before the attackers noticed him, Cal raised his weapon. *Bam. Bam. Bam.*

Her eyes widened. With just three shots, three of the black-scarved men fell to the ground. They were all clutching their shoulders.

Shouting and confusion erupted. The archeologists all sprung to their feet. Cal rushed forward and slammed the butt of his gun into the final attacker's shocked face. The man tried to fight back, but a second later he was unconscious on the ground.

Dani moved in now, too. She spotted one of the men Cal had shot fumbling for his weapon. She raced over and pressed the tip of the machete to the man's neck. "I wouldn't."

Angry, dark eyes glared up at her.

She reached down, grabbed the handgun and tossed it away. She looked up and saw Cal checking the other men and divesting them of any weapons. He pulled some black zip ties from his pocket, and set about tying the men up.

She blinked as she watched him. This was a man she didn't know. This the skilled, well-trained soldier. A man who'd risked his life to protect others.

He stood, his gaze running over her before he

looked at the archeologists. "Everyone okay? Anyone hurt?"

They looked a little battered. Sam had an arm around a disheveled Gemma. Jean-Luc was helping Dr. Oakley to his feet.

"Oakley?" Cal asked. "You took a punch."

The older archeologist waved a hand. "I'm fine. A little tender, that's all."

"Everyone sure they're okay?" Cal asked again.

The team nodded.

"The way you took those guys down..." Sam shook his head. "You are badass, man."

"Badass is my job, Sam."

Dr. Oakley cleared his throat. "Thank you, Cal."

"That's what I'm here for." He turned to look at the attackers. "Jean-Luc, Sakada, there is another one of these guys tied up on the other side of the temple. Bring him around." Cal glanced their way. "He was out cold. You might need to carry him."

Jean-Luc nodded. "We will get him."

Cal studied their attackers. "Why did you attack us?"

The men all stared at the ground.

"They're opportunists, right?" Gemma said. "Looking for some quick cash?"

"I don't think so," Cal said in an icy tone that raised the hairs on the back of Dani's neck. "Why did you attack us?"

One of the men lifted his head, his dark eyes burning. "Fuck you."

Cal crouched, lifting his handgun. "Who do you work for?"

The man looked belligerently over Cal's shoulder. Dani felt her stomach tighten. She got the feeling these weren't simple bandits.

"Do you work for Silk Road?" Cal asked.

Silk Road? Everything in Dani went cold. She'd heard of them, especially their ruthless attack on the dig in Egypt in an attempt to capture the oasis of Zerzura.

The man uttered something in another language. Even though she didn't know what it meant, she knew it was a curse.

Cal sighed. "The hard way, then."

\*\*\*

Cal stomped through the jungle, his mind whirling.

He'd had no luck getting their attackers to talk. They'd clammed up and said nothing. He'd left them tied up and bleeding, but that didn't soothe his nerves.

There was more to the attack. He was sure of it. He'd tried to contact Darcy but hadn't had any luck getting a satellite connection.

Dani appeared at his shoulder. "It'll be dark soon."

"Yeah. We'll make camp shortly."

"You're angry."

He pulled in a breath. "I wanted to find out what those men wanted."

"You don't think they were just after valuables?"

"No."

She sighed. "Me neither."

Cal detected something in her voice. "What is it?"

"One of them...I'm pretty sure he was the man who attacked me in Siem Reap and tried to snatch my camera."

*Fuck.* Cal's jaw clenched. He wasn't surprised. "I need to call my office." He'd climb a tree if he had to.

"You really think they're Silk Road?" she asked.

He stilled. "What do you know about Silk Road?"

"Only what's been in the press."

"I don't know for sure, but Silk Road is dangerous. You don't want to mess with them."

They'd reached a small clearing. It would have to do. He turned to face the others. "We'll set up camp here for the night. Sam, slash some of this undergrowth away. Everyone else, get your tents up. Eat, rest."

Once everyone was busy, Cal pulled out his satellite phone. He had a fifty-fifty chance the thing would work in this clearing. Jungles and satellite phones were not the best of friends.

When he turned it on, it was showing signal. He punched in the THS office number and waited.

"God, Cal, I've been trying to contact you all day." Darcy's harried voice came through, a little crackly, but clear.

"What's going on, D?"

"I got a call from Agent Arrogant and Annoying."

Cal choked back a laugh. Darcy's dislike of Special Agent Alastair Burke from the FBI's Art Crime Team was legendary. "What did he do to piss you off now?"

"Breathe," she said tartly. "But he sent me through some info. He got a ping on the passports of some people his team have been monitoring. People he suspects work for Silk Road."

Cal's gut went hard. Looked like his instincts had been right.

"Forty-eight hours ago, these people entered Cambodia. Their boss, a woman named Raven, has been in the country for two weeks. Burke says the rumor is they're after some ancient artifact in the jungle."

The hairs on the back of Cal's neck rose. "Fuck. D, my group was attacked a couple of hours ago. No one's hurt...except the attackers. They were trying to look like thieves out to rob us, but I knew there was something off about them."

"Cal, you need to be careful." He could hear his sister tapping on a keyboard. "Have your archeologists mentioned any valuable artifacts? Silk Road doesn't go for stone statues and ruined temples. They want rare, unique, and priceless."

"Nothing like that. An old temple that's probably falling to pieces."

"You need help." More tapping. "I'm contacting Logan and Morgan now. I'll have them there as soon as I can."

Other than Declan, Cal couldn't think of two people he'd prefer to have at his back in a fight. "Okay. Hopefully it'll be nothing, and we'll have blown money on flights for nothing."

"Hopefully," Darcy said, doubt coloring her voice.

"Okay, my darling D. I have to go."

"Take care of yourself, Callum. And don't miss your next scheduled check-in. If you're even a minute late, I'm sending in an army."

"Roger that."

A short while later, he stood, his back against a tree, munching on a pre-packed meal, and listening to the archeologists talking. They had a small, battery-powered lantern set up, and they were huddled around it. They seemed to be recovering from the attack.

Dani moved out of the darkness. "Wow, it is really dark in the jungle."

Cal nodded. "You did well today, when we were attacked."

"Thanks."

He grabbed her arm. "But you shouldn't have argued with me. You should have listened and stayed safe."

In the dim light, he saw her stubborn chin lift. "You may as well save your breath."

Yeah, he figured she was going to say something like that. "I don't want you hurt."

He felt the tension in her muscles ease a little. "Did your sister have any news?"

"Yes. Several Silk Road mercenaries are in the country and looking for an artifact in the jungle. They're thieves who are known to stop at nothing to get their hands on valuable artifacts."

She was quiet for a second. "What would they want with a ruined temple?"

"That's the question of the day." He

straightened. "You should get some rest. We have another big day tomorrow."

"And you? Are you going to rest?"

"I'll catch a few hours. Goodnight, Dani. Sleep well." He watched her walk away. He wasn't planning to sleep. He was going to stay on guard through the night.

If Silk Road was out here and after his group, they were going to have to go through him to get to them.

# Chapter Six

Logan O'Connor sat at the bar, nursing a beer, the clack of balls on the pool tables behind him.

Someone moved up beside him.

"Hey there. Looking for some company?"

He turned and looked at the woman. Generous curves, a cloud of brown hair, and a wide smile.

"Nope." He lifted his beer.

The woman regrouped and leaned against the bar. "Oh, come on. Everyone likes to have some fun."

Yeah, once he had. Once he'd been dumb enough to fall for a pretty face and a lush body. It had almost cost him his life and had cost a good man the ability to walk.

"I said no," he growled.

The woman made a sound. "No need to be rude." She stormed off.

"Another one bites the dust." Morgan slid onto the stool beside him.

"Not interested."

"You know, beneath all your wild and shaggy, there's a good man in there somewhere. A good woman might smooth out those rough edges of yours."

Logan took another long drag of his beer. He was grateful he didn't have any sisters. Between Morgan and Darcy, he had all the meddling women he could handle.

"We could get started on you not having a man."

Morgan sniffed. "I haven't found one who can keep up with me."

Logan grunted. He felt his cell phone vibrate in his pocket a second before it started ringing. He pulled it out. "O'Connor."

"Logan, thank God." Darcy's worried voice.

Logan pushed his beer away and straightened. "What is it?"

"I need you and Morgan to get to the airport. I've organized a commercial flight for you both to Cambodia. The jet's on the East Coast to pick up Ronin and Hale."

She was talking a mile a minute. "Slow down. Take a breath."

"It's Cal. He needs help. Silk Road is in Cambodia and they attacked his team. They're all right, but he needs help."

*Shit.* "You're sure it's Silk Road?"

Darcy's voice soured. "Agent Know-it-all contacted me. He passed the info along. We have no idea what they're after, but Logan, I've got a really bad feeling about this."

Logan nodded his head toward the door and Morgan slid off her stool. "Morgan's with me. We'll spin by our places, grab our gear, and get to the airport." Moments later, he was striding across the bar parking lot toward his truck. "Don't worry, we'll get there as soon as we can. And Cal's tough, smart, and fast. He can keep ahead of Silk Road."

He heard Darcy swallow. "I know."

Logan unlocked his truck and climbed inside. Morgan slid into the passenger seat. He started the engine. "Darcy, you work your magic. Have a vehicle and gear waiting for us when we land. We'll get to the jungle and find Cal."

She pulled in a deep breath. "I know you're worried, too. You haven't even bitched about going to the jungle."

"Hate the mosquitos. And the humidity sucks, too."

Darcy let out a small laugh. "Okay, okay, don't start. Find him, Logan."

Logan gunned his truck out of the parking lot. "Count on it."

***

Cal slashed at the vines. He was a little gritty-eyed this morning, but he was used to going without sleep.

The archeologists had bounced back after a good night's sleep, and seemed to have shrugged off yesterday's attack. They were following behind him, their conversation upbeat.

They knew they'd reach the temple soon.

He glanced back and saw Dani bringing up the rear. She'd braided her hair today, and more than anything, he wanted to tear that hair tie out and work those curls between his hands.

With a muttered curse, he turned back to the jungle. He had to have the woman soon, or desire was going to drive him out of his mind.

He cut through some more vines and undergrowth. At least, there'd been no sign of anyone else in the jungle with them. He was praying this entire Silk Road thing was nothing.

Then he pulled up short.

He'd stumbled onto a clearing.

Sunlight shone down on a stone arch, with the trees growing over the top of it. Beyond the arch there appeared to be a pathway.

He paused. It was moments like this that made his job rewarding. Discovering these things that no one had seen for hundreds or thousands of years.

"God." A grinning Gemma pushed forward. "Guys, look at this."

"It has to be the path leading to the temple," Sakada said. "We must not have much farther to go."

Sam stepped forward, studying his map. "We don't. It looks like the temple is down that stone pathway."

They continued on. Cal strapped his machete to his belt. The stone pathway was uneven now, and the jungle vegetation was growing through and around it. But it meant the plant life hadn't grown as thickly here.

He could hear Dani's camera clicking as she captured every moment.

They kept moving, and then he heard gasps from the team.

He looked up and felt his chest tighten. Hell, he hadn't even noticed it at first. The entire temple was overgrown with green vegetation.

It was as tall as the trees and shaped like a step pyramid. Damn. It looked more like the Mayan pyramids Cal had seen in Central America, than the temples of Angkor. Each of the five levels was smaller than the one before it, covered in a carpet of green vegetation.

"This makes every boring dig I've ever been on worth it," Gemma murmured.

The others all broke out into laughter and ecstatic exclamations. They all hurried forward toward the ruined temple.

Even Dani was grinning from behind the camera.

"It looks like the seven-tier pyramid of Prasat Thom at Koh Ker," Sakada said, his gaze glued to the temple. "This one is smaller, of course, but the design is similar."

"It is amazing." Dr. Oakley glanced at Cal. "We need to get inside."

Cal hacked away more vegetation, and led them to the doorway at the center of what he guessed was the front of the temple. He looked up, marveling again at the construction.

Dr. Oakley's shoulders drooped. "It's blocked up with rocks."

Rubble filled the entrance. "Sam, can you give me a hand?" Cal gripped one of the large rocks. Sam grabbed the other end and together they heaved the boulder away. Sakada and Jean-Luc followed suit with the next rock.

They quickly found a rhythm of heaving and rolling, and were soon making progress.

"Mmm, nothing like watching strong men flexing their muscles and lifting heavy things," Gemma said.

Sam grunted. "You could come and help. I'm all for gender equality."

Gemma sniffed. "I'm not sure hauling rocks is going to help with women's rights."

Cal ignored them and focused on the entry. He could see a gap through the rocks. "Not much more, and we'll be able to get through."

It took a little more lifting and straining, but they finally cleared a space large enough to enter.

Dr. Oakley had pulled out flashlights, and eagerly stepped forward, flicking on the strong beam of light.

The other archeologists moved in behind him. As they exclaimed at the engravings on the walls, their excitement was palpable.

Cal grinned at Dani. "Feels pretty good, huh?"

She nodded, taking a few more shots of the darkened entrance. "This is my first lost temple. I'm usually trying to take pictures around the tourists...this is amazing." She lifted the camera again.

Cal reached up and pushed it back down. Her gaze met his. "Experience it without the camera, first. Just for a minute. Look at the carvings, here." He ran his hand over the faint engravings bordering the doorway. "No one has seen these for hundreds of years. We're making history, Dani."

Her gaze drifted over the wall.

"Stop thinking about getting the perfect shot. What do you *feel*?"

"Excited. Exhilarated. Energized."

Exactly how he felt. And all of it was revolving around the woman in front of him. He touched the shell of her ear. "Good, isn't it? It makes you feel alive. What we feel, that's really all we have." He backed her up a few steps, until her back hit the rock wall.

Her breathing increased, her chest rising and falling against his. Her gaze never left his.

"Emotions can be fleeting, Cal. Excitement, lust, desire, love… Here one minute, gone the next. And afterward, you're left with nothing."

He pressed his hands to the wall on either side of her head. "It doesn't have to be that way." He lowered his head until his lips were a breath away from hers. "Right here, right this instant, it's just you and me. No camera between us, no one else to get in the way." He lowered his voice. "I want you, Dani. So damn much."

She made a sound and threw her arms around his shoulders. Her mouth slammed against his.

With a groan, he thrust his tongue into her mouth and pulled her close. He moved a thigh between her legs, feeling the warmth of her against him. God, she kissed with a hunger that set him on fire. He yanked his lips from hers and pressed a trail of kisses down her neck. The scent of her filled him and, helpless to stop himself, he nipped at her skin, and when she made choked little moans, he smiled.

"Cal? Dani? Where are you guys?"

Dr. Oakley's voice was like a splash of cold water.

Cal pulled back, willing his hammering pulse to slow. "Later." It was a promise he intended to keep. Something in him was very hungry for this woman, and it wouldn't be held off much longer.

She lifted her chin, her eyes hot. "Later."

As she headed down the tunnel into the temple, Cal took a second to adjust himself. His cock was hard as iron. A second later, he followed her.

\*\*\*

Dani stepped out of the entrance tunnel and into an open room.

A gasp tangled in her throat. The entire inside of the pyramid was hollow. One large room, where all the walls were engraved with fabulous scenes—undamaged, and in beautiful condition.

She was reeling—both from the temple discovery and Cal's kiss. The man was right. She felt incredibly alive.

Hearing him behind her and excruciatingly aware of his presence, she lifted her camera. It was time to get to work and put her distractions aside. As he moved up beside her, bumping his shoulder against hers, she realized just how hard it was to put her number one distraction out of her mind. A man like Callum Ward was hard to ignore.

But as she focused on the fantastic engravings on the wall of the temple, it didn't take long for her to fall into the groove of taking her shots. She moved around the temple, taking pictures of the brilliant artwork, engraved with such care and dedication.

She turned the camera on the team. God...their faces. Jean-Luc looked like he wanted to sit down and pray. Dr. Oakley was smiling, his countenance filled with reverence. Gemma was busy scribbling notes, Sam taking photos, and Sakada was focused on deciphering the text.

Drawn to the fabulous bas-reliefs on the wall—of sensuous dancing women, incredible beasts, and fearsome naga—Dani burned through her memory card. She stopped to slot another one in. She could stay in here all day, capturing the art on the walls. She wished for some better light, but she could work with what she had. She imagined these walls had a story to tell, and she longed to decipher the images and text.

She moved along the walls, taking shots of everything. At the back wall of the temple, she paused. Intricate images of people with elaborate headdresses, all seated with their legs crossed, larger gods, and amazing beasts—lions, deer and some animals she couldn't identify—all filled the walls. They circled the image of a large, oval-shaped stone. The mythical linga of Mahendraparvata.

She worked her way back around, and then she noticed Cal, leaning against the wall with his arms crossed over his chest, watching the team intently.

Dani snapped a shot of him—that tough, serious face. She realized now he was quick to smile and charm, but as the images of him fighting those men who'd attacked them flashed in her head, she now knew he could also be serious and deadly. An intriguing contrast.

She followed his gaze and studied the team. They were huddled together, whispering quietly. None of them were smiling. Sakada was waving at one wall of engravings.

She sidled up beside Cal. "What's up?"

"What do you mean?"

"Ward, I may not have known you long, but I'm getting pretty good at reading that face of yours."

He scraped his fingers over his stubble-covered jaw. "What do you see when you look at them?"

She turned with a frown. "You mean the team?"

"Yeah. I guess I expected them to be more…elated. We trekked all this way to find this temple, but they look—"

"Disappointed." The word came out of Dani without thinking. She looked down at her camera, flicking through her last few images. She saw the disappointment and frustration she'd caught on their faces.

Cal nodded and raised his voice. "Dr. Oakley, you want to tell me what the problem is?"

The archeologist turned, pushing his glasses up his nose. "Sorry? I don't know what you—"

Cal pushed away from the wall. "You're a terrible liar, doc. Tell me why you guys are so disappointed with the lost temple you just discovered."

Tiredly, Dr. Oakley nodded and waved the rest of the team over. They all perched on lumps of rock, except for Gemma, who dropped to the stone floor and crossed her legs. Dani leaned against the wall and waited.

"This is the Temple of the Sacred Linga. From what we have researched...well, we'd hoped to actually *find* the linga here."

Cal raised a brow. "You turning treasure hunter on me, doc? You were really hoping to find some mythical stone with magical powers?"

"Okay, it sounds stupid when you say it like that." Dr. Oakley's tone was dry.

Gemma leaned forward, resting her elbows on her knees. "There were hints. From the other temples we've studied, it seemed there was a good chance the linga was going to be here. From how it's described, we think it's some sort of giant pearl. Its value—both historic and monetary—would be immense."

Cal's gaze ran over them. "Dammit, you should have told me about this before. And? There's something else, isn't there?"

Sakada took a deep breath. "We've been scouring all the legends of my country, of the Hindu religion. We believe the sacred linga of Mahendraparvata, the stone that possessed the power to create an entire empire, is the cintamani stone."

Dani frowned. She'd never heard the word before.

Cal was frowning too. "What's the cintamani stone?"

It was Sakada who answered. "It is a revered stone in Hindu and Buddhist tradition. A fabulous jewel that grants the wishes of whoever holds it."

Gemma smiled. "It's the equivalent of the Philosopher's stone. Some believe the stones to be one and the same."

Cal crossed his arms over his chest. "And you think a fabulous, mystical jewel is sitting in a lost temple in Cambodia?"

Dr. Oakley leaned forward. "We didn't set out to prove the Mahendraparvata linga was the famed cintamani. But as we did our research, more and more things fell into place. Once Sakada suggested the linga was actually the cintamani, the more facts we found to confirm it."

Gemma leaned back, her face alive with excitement. "The cintamani was said to be in the possession of the naga king."

A muscle in Cal's jaw ticked. "The same naga king whose daughter birthed the Cambodian people?"

"That's right," Jean-Luc said. "The stone is often described as resting on the forehead of a makara."

"The sea monster," Dani said.

"And," Dr. Oakley said, "the cintamani stone is said to be a large pearl. Just like the Mahendraparvata linga."

Cal shook his head. "I've been on a lot of expeditions and provided security for a lot of digs. You guys know this better than me, but most of the time you don't find much left. What are the chances this valuable jewel would still be here?"

Dr. Oakley's smile was a little sad. "Slim. But an archeologist can dream."

Gemma stretched her legs out. "Come on, Cal. History says the cintamani can grant your greatest wish…doesn't it make you want to believe?"

Cal snorted. "If I want something, I go out and get it. I'm not going to wait around hoping some mystical stone will grant it for me." Everyone laughed but Cal's serious face had the laughter dying out. "You should have told me about the cintamani. There's a chance someone else got wind of it."

Dani's chest hitched. "You're talking about the attackers."

He nodded. "And the man who tried to snatch your camera in Siem Reap. A very bad group of people believe your crazy theory is true and are after the cintamani, as well."

The archeologists traded glances.

"We haven't shared our information with anyone," Sakada said.

"Nor have we kept it a secret," Dr. Oakley added with a frown. "But it doesn't appear that the stone is here." He looked around the elaborate walls. "Let's hope your suspicions are incorrect, Cal, and these people realize there is nothing to find."

"Yes, let's hope."

Dani didn't think Cal sounded that hopeful.

"Any more secrets I should know about?" Cal asked.

They all shook their heads.

"While we don't have a sacred stone, we still have a fabulous, undocumented temple to investigate and record." Dr. Oakley clapped his hands together. "I think it's time we get to work."

"Right." Gemma stood, dusting off her trousers. "We need photos, measurements, translations. And I'm guessing Dani will want some more shots as well."

Dani lifted her camera. "Absolutely."

"Well, get to work." Cal looked at his rugged watch. "I'll keep a watch outside, and get our camp set up." He shot Dani a look, one that turned hot. "Stay out of trouble."

# Chapter Seven

Cal finished setting up the tents. They had a small fire going and most of the archeologists were now sitting around it, talking about the temple, laughing and eating the pre-packaged food they'd brought along. The fire was more for ambience than anything else, casting a warm glow around the camp.

But as thunder rumbled overhead, and the darkness grew, he figured the fire wasn't going to last too much longer.

He'd already organized for each member of the team to take a shift on watch through the night. Their encounter with Silk Road had left him wary. But he was in desperate need of some sleep and couldn't spend another night awake, so that meant everyone was going to do two-hour shifts. And Cal was keeping his SIG close.

He watched the firelight flicker over Dani's face. She was munching on something from her backpack, and nodding at something Gemma was saying to her. The light did magnificent things to her cheekbones, and he found himself staring.

He couldn't remember the last time he was so drawn to a particular woman. And it wasn't just what she looked like. He liked her smart mouth, her talent and dedication for her work, her smile.

Cal grabbed his bottle of water and took a long drink.

"So...where did this cintamani stone come from?" Dani asked.

Dr. Oakley leaned forward, cradling his drink bottle. "No one knows for sure. There are lots of myths."

"Buddhist legend says four sacred relics fell from the sky and one was the cintamani," Sakada said.

"Another myth says the stone came from the undersea kingdom of the naga," Jean-Luc added.

"It has even been linked to Chinese mythology." Gemma's voice rose as she told her story. "Some believe that the cintamani came from the mythological Kunlun Mountains. A sacred mountain, dwelling place of the gods and goddesses. It was said to be a place of marvelous, bejeweled plants, gem-like rocks, and strange creatures, perhaps home to the revered Eight Immortals of Chinese legend."

Jean-Luc made a scoffing sound. "The Kunlun Mountains are pure myth. They didn't really exist."

"Oh?" Gemma's eyes lit up. "And yet the Kunlun Mountains were linked to Mount Meru, sacred mountain mythology revered here in Cambodia. Embodied in that very temple." She stabbed a finger at the temple looming nearby. "Even Angkor Wat is built in the image of the sacred mountain. Who's to say that Kunlun Mountain, which is associated with the old Khmer word for King of the

Mountains, isn't linked to *Kulen* mountain, right here where we are?"

"Come on, Gemma." The French archeologist shook his head. "You don't really believe that."

"Maybe I do. There is also the story of the Russian explorer back in the early 1900s who traveled through Asia. He claimed to be gifted a fragment of the cintamani by a high abbot of a monastery."

The others all groaned.

Cal watched Dani, who was watching the exchange with fascination. Good-natured arguments like this were the mainstay of his family. His mother was always going on about the latest crack-pot theory or conspiracy. His father patiently stated the facts. And usually Cal, Dec and Darcy got a few teasing comments in, here and there. Knowing what he did about Dani's family, he figured this wasn't something she saw much.

Dr. Oakley smiled. "Next, you'll claim it was created by aliens."

Gemma sniffed. "That explorer said he was told the cintamani was linked to the Eight Immortals from the Kunlun Mountains."

"Hogwash," Jean-Luc said.

"No one actually uses *hogwash*, Jean-Luc," Gemma said.

"It's all really fascinating," Dani said. "Whatever the truth, that there can be this much history and mystery around one stone is amazing."

Cal felt a fat drop of water land on his hand. He looked up as a huge lightning strike lit the sky beyond the trees. "Hope no one minds getting wet."

There were good-natured grumbles. Sam snatched up his tablet and made a bee-line for his tent. The archeologists grabbed their things and followed suit. Jean-Luc nodded at Cal. "I'll be ready to do the first watch tonight."

"Thanks, Jean-Luc. If you see or hear anything that worries you, wake me."

Dani pulled a lightweight, waterproof coat on and made sure her camera was covered. She grabbed one of the battery-powered lanterns but didn't head for her tent.

"Where are you going?"

She looked back over her shoulder. "I want to get a few more shots inside the temple. Don't worry, Dad, I won't go far."

"It'll be too dark in the temple for photos."

She lifted the lantern. "I want to get some creative shots in the lantern light." As the rain started to thunder down, she broke into a jog.

Cal did a quick lap of the camp, and checked that everyone was safely settled for the night. He was pretty certain the Silk Road goons they'd tangled with would be too busy taking care of their injuries to risk following them. Still, he'd be happier when Logan and Morgan arrived.

By the time he ducked inside the temple, his hair was saturated, his wet shirt clinging to his skin. When he stepped into the main area, the lantern cast a golden glow in the space. Dani looked up and lowered her camera. "Rain's coming down?"

At that moment, thunder crashed overhead. "You could say that." When her gaze lingered on his chest, he was more than pleased. He felt his pulse spike.

She looked back at the engraved wall. "It's just so beautiful. I don't know...something about it just calls to me. I wanted to make sure I captured all the carvings on the four walls." She reached out and touched the image of a naga. The fierce, snake-like creature was coiled on the bottom, its head rearing up.

"Something about you has been calling to me ever since you were rude to me at Angkor Wat."

She turned slowly and he saw her hands clench on her camera. Their eyes locked. The space between them seemed to throb and Cal felt a ball of desire ignite in his gut.

"Cal—"

He stalked toward her. She was as still as the carvings on the wall, watching him come.

He stopped a foot away. "Moment of truth, Dani. You going to keep running, or let me have you?" He closed another few inches, until her camera bumped against his chest. "Are you going to stop denying what you feel, and follow your instincts?"

He kept his gaze on her. Wanting to watch every emotion skitter across her face.

She pulled in a shaky breath. "I've spent my life following my head..."

Cal reached out and gripped the camera. Gently, he lifted it over her head and set it down on a nearby block of stone. "No camera, Dani. No shield.

No ghosts from the past." He backed her up against the wall, until his chest was pressed hard against hers. Desire was a primal need pounding through him, matching the drumming of the wild storm he heard outside. He tangled his fingers with hers. "Just feel."

The kiss was desperate, hungry, with an edge that had them both moaning. Then Dani made a hot, eager sound, and Cal felt her hands tugging his wet shirt out of the waistband of his trousers. God, that sound made him harder.

She jerked her head back. "Skin. I want skin."

He helped her, and then felt the slide of her palms up his abdomen, the scrape of her nails on his chest.

He attacked the fastening on her trousers, and her mouth slid along his jaw, her teeth sinking into his earlobe. He growled against her.

"This is crazy," she murmured. "But God, I want you."

It was crazy. Desire was a huge, reckless rush inside him. Finally, he worked his hand inside her trousers. He slipped past the elastic of her panties and cupped the damp warmth of her.

"God, Dani, you're so wet."

She moaned against him, her mouth pressed to his chest now. Her hips moved against his hand, and he worked one finger through her curls and slid it inside her.

Chest heaving, he kept sliding inside her, and moved his thumb until he found her clit. He watched, drinking in the emotions on her face as she arched back and cried out.

"Do you like that, beautiful?"

"Yes." It came out a hiss.

This time, he slid a second finger inside her. Damn, she was tight. "Tell me how it feels."

"Full." Her chest hitched. "Stretched."

"You'll feel it more when my cock's inside you. But right now, I want to watch you come, Dani."

He worked her harder, faster, was rougher than he wanted to be. With his other hand, he yanked the tie from her hair and watched her dark curls spill around her shoulders.

That look on her face, the flush on her cheeks, the rapid rise and fall of her chest…he felt the insane and unfamiliar urge to take, possess, and own.

He pinched her clit between his fingers and she cried out, her body shuddering through her orgasm.

Cal had never seen anything more perfect. "Damn, I want to be inside you."

A breath shuddered out of her, and her eyes were still a little unfocused. "I want you inside me, too."

Cal's cock throbbed, almost painful. He groaned. "Not here, beautiful." Not in the dust and dirt. "When we get back to Siem Reap, I'm going to show you how good it can be. Stretched out on a big bed with clean sheets. I'm not taking you hard and fast against some stone wall." He cupped her face, pushing her hair back. He could smell the musky scent of her on his fingers. "Soon. You'd better be ready."

"Yes," she murmured.

He groaned and forced himself to take a step back. "Come on, we should get back before I fuck you here in the dirt."

He saw a shiver go through her, and she glanced at the temple doorway. "It's still bucketing down." Her gaze came back to him, before flicking downward.

He knew she couldn't miss the hard outline of his cock straining against the front of his trousers.

She licked her lips.

He groaned. "God…don't look at me like that. I won't be held responsible for my actions."

This time, it was Dani who nudged him back, with a surprisingly strong push. He felt rock hit the back of his knees and sat down on a large stone block. Next thing he knew, her hands were at his belt. Vicious need raked his gut and more blood surged into his cock. "Dani—"

"Shh. I'll keep you to the promise of that big bed. But that doesn't mean I can't help you out right now."

"Just because I made you come doesn't mean you have to return the favor, Dani. I didn't do it for that reason."

Those unique bi-colored eyes met his. "I know. I *want* to touch you."

Cal let out a tortured groan. "You mean bring me to my knees. I'm already there, beautiful."

The smile she shot him went straight to his cock. It was all secrets and sex. "You're not there yet, Cal. But you will be."

She reached inside his trousers and boxers and pulled out his cock. She made a humming sound.

Shit, he was in trouble. She wrapped her hands around him and started stroking. No hesitation or delicacy. Soon, his hips were jerking up toward her firm touch. He gritted his teeth against the wild sensation. God, he really wanted to tear her clothes off and take her, like some primitive caveman staking his claim.

His blood pounded through his veins. "Dani—"

Suddenly her hands were gone. He barely swallowed back his protest. She stepped back a little, her face flushed, her chest rising and falling. "Touch yourself." A sensual whisper. "Show me how you do it."

He circled his cock with a firm grip and pumped. He didn't look down, instead, he watched the way her gaze was glued to his movements, the way her lips parted and more color filled her cheeks. Yeah, his girl was getting off on this.

"Are you getting wet again?"

Her gaze flicked up to his face. "Yes."

"You want me inside you, don't you? You want this—" he slid his hand down, baring the swollen head of his cock "—inside you. Filling up that slick wetness?"

She licked her lips again. "Yes." Her hand moved over his, and together, they pumped his cock. Cal could feel his orgasm growing like a fire at the base of his spine.

She moved her hand over the head of his cock, her finger moving through the slit and smearing his pre-come over his sensitive skin. His hips jerked again, completely out of his control. His breathing was labored, and he kept his gaze on those slim fingers stroking him.

Her hands wrapped around him, tightened, and she pressed her body into his side. He felt her lips at his throat.

"Come for me, Cal. I want to watch."

*Fuck.* The need to come was a brutal clawing in his gut. And a second later he did, his muscles locking and his vision dimming. His come spilled over their joined hands and across his belly. He groaned, long and loud. Then her mouth landed on his and he kissed her deeply.

Slowly, he came back down and pressed his forehead to hers. Then, there was only the steady beat of the rain and their fast breathing.

"Well—" her voice sounded a little shaky.

"When we get back to the hotel, I'm coming to your hotel room. I'm going to lock the door and spend hours—hell, days—fucking you. That's your only warning."

She trembled.

And then, as though someone had turned off a faucet, the rain cut off. Dani stepped back, her gaze still on him. "Well, we seem to have made a little mess. I have some wipes in my pocket." She pulled them out and handed him one. "I keep them for cleaning my camera."

It only took him a minute to clean up and tuck himself back into his trousers. He pulled her into his arms and held her there. Right now he wanted the contact, needed it.

"Come on. I'll get you back to your tent. It's bedtime and, unfortunately, it looks like we're both going to bed alone."

She looked up at him again, and he growled.

"I told you not to look at me like that." He slapped her on the butt, snagged her camera, and handed it back to her. "Let's get moving, Navarro."

The rain had stopped, but water still dripped off the foliage above. The camp was dark and quiet. When they reached the tents, they paused, looking at each other.

He pressed his lips to hers. A gentler kiss than they'd shared so far. "Dream of me."

"Oh, I have no doubt about that," she murmured. Then she ducked inside her tent.

Cal did another lap of the camp and the surroundings, checking in with Jean-Luc who was soon handing over the watch to Sam. Cal also searched for any sign they had unwanted company. Everything was quiet.

When he finally made his way back to his tent, he lifted his face to the sky. A cold drip of water came off a tree. He wished it was a cold shower.

***

Hours later, Cal flopped back on his sleeping bag and stared at the roof of his tent.

He'd dozed for a couple of hours, but now he couldn't sleep. He was tired from the long day and the sleepless night the evening before, but his cock was hard, desire humming through his veins. He was pretty sure he wasn't getting any sleep anytime soon. Images of what he and Dani had done in the temple kept flashing through his head. He could hear her cries, smell the musky scent of her, taste her on his lips.

He groaned and threw an arm over his face. It was pretty hard to forget that she was only one tent away from him.

The fact that they could have done more in the temple, that he could have slid inside her tight warmth, taunted him. He'd never been one to turn aside a fast, hard quickie.

But for the first time in his life, he wanted to take his time with a woman. He wanted to take his time to enjoy her, to bring her pleasure. He knew she hadn't had that before. She'd seen fast and meaningless...Cal wanted to give her more. Like he'd told her, he wanted the big bed, hell, maybe even a bottle of champagne.

Oh yeah, he could imagine spilling the golden liquid down her naked body and taking his time to lap it up.

Eventually, despite the X-rated fantasies running through his head, he dozed off. When he woke, it was still dark and his body clock told him he hadn't been asleep very long. He stayed still, wondering what had woken him.

He heard another sound. A footstep. He frowned. Probably Dr. Oakley who'd taken over the watch a short while ago. Or Gemma sneaking into Sam's tent. Those two were doing a pretty poor job of hiding the fact they were banging each other.

But when he heard a sound again, he let his instincts lead. He was still wary after the other attack.

Cal pulled his boots on silently, and very slowly, he unzipped his tent. He crept out into the darkness, only hearing normal jungle sounds now. Whoever was moving around out here hadn't frightened the animals.

Which meant they were either not a threat, or damn good at sneaking around.

He circled around behind his tent, straining to see anything through the thick darkness. The last thing he needed to do was burst in on Sam and Gemma.

He saw shadows on the other side of camp and he crouched and went still. He couldn't make out who it was.

A second later, gunfire broke through the night.

Cal cursed, pulled out his SIG Sauer and moved back a bit, deeper into the shadows. The urge to get to Dani's tent was strong, and he had to wrestle it back. He needed more intel first. Who was attacking them, how many were there, and what the hell were they after?

He took a second to reach into his tent and grab his backpack. He always kept a few supplies in it, in case of emergency. He crept away, ducked behind some thicker undergrowth, and waited.

Flashlights flicked on and he heard shouts. A large group of people was going through the camp, pulling his team from their tents. A bedraggled

Jean-Luc, a frightened Sakada, and a belligerent Dr. Oakley were thrust onto their knees near the now-dead fire. A cursing Sam and a screaming Gemma followed. Cal saw Dani struggling against a larger man as he dragged her toward the others. Her camera dangled against her chest. She got in a good hit to his gut before he shook her hard and dumped her on the ground.

Cal's hands flexed on his weapon. He wanted to rush in. He wanted to take down the guy so badly.

He forced himself to breathe. To do his job. If he rushed in there, he'd be dead in a second. Then they'd all be dead.

He fought for some calm, trying to think things through. He made himself track all the attackers. Six standing in the center of the camp. At least three more moving around the perimeter. Cal thrust his hand into the damp earth beneath him, like that would hold him there. He needed to wait for the right opportunity.

With reluctance dragging on him, he melted into the jungle trees. Trying to feel like he wasn't abandoning them, failing them, like he had his best friend.

Cal circled around, catching glimpses of the invaders through the trees. These guys were professionals. They had the archeology team all on their knees, hands behind their heads. A few of the attackers were going through the tents, tearing things apart.

A lean man strode out of the jungle, flanked by two more thugs. He paused to give quiet orders to the rest of his group. Two of the men nodded and hurried off to obey whatever order had been given. Cal focused on the newcomer, trying to hear what he was saying. When the man turned, his face illuminated by the beam from one of the flashlights, Cal realized it wasn't a man. It was a woman.

The woman stepped forward, her gaze on the archeologists. Her lean, athletic body was encased in snug, black leggings and a fitted black shirt. Her red hair was pulled back tight off her face, highlighting razor-sharp cheekbones and copper skin.

"Where's the stone?"

Her tone said she was used to giving orders. She had an accent, but it was too faint for Cal to work out what it was.

Dr. Oakley stirred. "Who are you? You have no right to—"

"Save it," the woman said. "Answer my question."

"Stone?"

"Don't play dumb with me, Dr. Oakley." The woman crouched in front of the archeologist. She lifted her hand and light glinted off her handgun. She pressed the end of it under Dr. Oakley's jaw. "Where's the cintamani stone?"

Cal bit off a curse. He watched surprise flicker over Oakley's face.

"Lost to antiquity, I presume. It's not here. This is just a ruined temple."

The woman's mouth moved into a flat line. "My

intel tells me you were expecting to find it here."

"Intel?" Oakley looked baffled.

The woman's smile was almost friendly. "We've been following your team, Dr. Oakley. Watching your research."

"Who the hell are you?"

"We're a group just as interested in antiquities as you are."

A look flowed over Oakley's face. "Antiquities thieves."

The woman shrugged. "We aren't grave robbers or common criminals."

"You're Silk Road," Dani said.

The woman's head lifted. "Clever." Her cool gaze moved over the rest of the archeologists, who were all watching her with shock and dread. "I had the chance to *talk* with some of your team. I got valuable information off them about what you were looking for, and where you were headed."

Cal's jaw tightened. Dr. Oakley's body had tensed and he glanced at the others. "My team members are all dedicated professionals. There is no way any of them would have shared anything with you."

The woman's smile widened a little. "Oh, it must be lovely to live in that deluded little world where bad things and betrayal never happen." In a single, lithe move, she stood. "But don't worry, I slipped something in their drinks at a bar one evening. It...loosened their tongues a little."

Now the rest of the team looked horrified.

The woman sauntered past the team, her gaze

moving over Jean-Luc, Gemma, and Sakada, before coming to rest on Sam. "If you didn't find the stone here—" she reached down and stroked Sam's face "—then I know you were hoping to find a hint, a clue, maybe a map to where the cintamani might be resting."

Sam blanched. "I remember now. That bar we went to last week... I woke up with a splitting headache. I thought I'd had too much to drink."

"You were very happy to share that you suspected this temple was either the home of the stone or at least the gateway to the stone," the woman said.

Oakley stirred. "It's just a theory—"

"You're all wasting my time. Where do I find the stone?" The woman stepped back and then kicked Sam. The toe of her boot dug into his ribs. Sam fell over with a cry, cradling his chest.

Dani surged to her feet, standing between the woman and Sam. "Leave him alone."

*No.* Cal mentally urged Dani to get back down and stay quiet.

The woman spun, her eyes narrowing. Quick as a snake, she backhanded Dani in the face. The force of the blow sent Dani staggering.

*Fuck.* This was going to go south very quickly. What this woman and her people wanted, it wasn't here. And something told Cal there was no way she was going to leave witnesses alive.

The woman lifted her gun, aiming it at Dani's chest. "Well, if you haven't found any sign of the cintamani, or its present location, then you're of no use to me."

Cal surged upward. He broke out of the trees, lifting his weapon.

He fired.

The woman went down with a cry, blood spurting from her shoulder. Dammit. Cal had been aiming for the center of the chest, but she'd moved at the last second. She was wounded but not down.

Her men started firing, and the archeologists dived to the ground, screaming. It was chaos.

Cal swiveled, aimed, fired. He ducked and spun. *Bam. Bam. Bam.* Five down, seven to go.

The other Silk Road thugs were running for cover now. Cal crouched down behind a tent.

"Dani, everyone, flat on the ground. Stay down."

He crept around the tent and saw another attacker crouched down behind the neighboring tent. Quietly, Cal crept up behind him. The man turned at the last second, but Cal got in one vicious chop to the back of the man's neck. He fell on the ground and after another hit, was out cold. It took Cal a second to zip tie the man's hands.

Six down. But as Cal was closing in on the other attackers, he heard more gunshots tear through the night. He spun. Heard a high, pain-filled scream.

Dammit, no! He leaped forward, firing, running toward his group. He saw Jean-Luc on his knees, hands pressed to his chest, blood oozing between his fingers. The archeologist's eyes were wide, his face pale.

Dani was struggling with another attacker. She

kicked the man and he went down. Dani raced toward Jean-Luc.

Movement snagged Cal's attention. The Silk Road leader was back up...and she was aiming her gun at Dani.

Cal burst forward, his arms pumping as he sprinted toward them. "Stop!"

But the woman stayed focused on her target.

Heart hammering, Cal lifted his SIG, the movement slow, feeling as though he were moving through honey.

The woman fired.

Cal saw Dani's body jerk, heard her cry out.

*No!*

# Chapter Eight

God, it hurt. Dani pressed down hard on her left bicep, biting her lip to stop from crying out. She'd been shot.

But her frantic gaze went to Jean-Luc. He was slumped on the ground, blood covering his chest.

She'd gone from dreaming of Cal and the hot, heady moments in the temple to the middle of a war zone. And where the hell was Cal? Was he okay?

She glanced frantically around the clearing, and, as though she'd summoned him, she spotted him charging across the camp. The breath rushed out of her. He was okay. He threw something, just as a Silk Road attacker came out of nowhere, and tackled him to the ground.

Dani struggled to her feet. She had to help him. Then she heard something hit the ground in front of her. It glinted metallically in the faint light and rolled across the dirt.

Her gut went hard. A *grenade*.

Before she could do anything else, it exploded.

Gemma screamed, and someone else shouted. Smoke poured into the air and then Dani couldn't see anything. All that was visible were a few flashlight beams, illuminating the smoke.

She felt her way over to Jean-Luc and bumped into someone.

"Dani?"

"Dr. Oakley? Are you okay?"

"I...I think so."

"Jean-Luc's been shot in the chest. We need to stop the bleeding." She turned to the injured man. "Jean-Luc, you hanging in there?"

The man groaned. "Hurts."

"I know. Let us have a look."

She had to lean close to him, the smoke still thick in the air. Her stomach rolled. God, there was so much blood. Dani shrugged out of her long-sleeved shirt. She had a dark blue tank on underneath. She balled up her shirt and pressed it to the wound.

Jean-Luc groaned again.

"I know. I'm sorry."

Suddenly, gunfire sounded loudly nearby. Dani fell forward over Jean-Luc, felt Dr. Oakley crouch close beside them.

Then Cal appeared out of the smoke.

"Cal."

She saw relief flash in his eyes and he took a second to touch her cheek. "I need you all to get out of here. There are still four of these guys out there, plus their leader." With expert hands, he lifted the wadded shirt off Jean-Luc, his face hardening. "He needs medical help. As soon as possible." He slipped the fabric under the man's shirt to hold it in place. "Keep the pressure on." Then Cal pulled out Sam's tablet. "I managed to grab this. Take it and head that way." He handed it to Dr. Oakley and pointed. "Keep moving, and get back to the village and the bikes. Sam, Gemma, and Sakada are waiting for you in the trees."

Fear lodged in Dani's throat. "What are you going to do?"

His blue eyes were like chips of ice. "I'm going to take the rest of these assholes out so they don't follow us." He yanked her forward for a brief kiss. "I'll find you. Now go."

She watched him disappear into the smoke and she quelled the urge to go after him.

"Come on," she said to Dr. Oakley. Together, they managed to get Jean-Luc on his feet, and the three of them hobbled toward the trees.

Behind her, she heard more gunshots. Each one made her flinch.

*Stay safe, Cal.*

They found the others waiting.

"Quick." Sakada waved them into the dark jungle.

Sam took Dani's place beside Jean-Luc, and with a nod, Dani took the lead. "We need to get to the closest village and the bikes."

Dani pushed vines and branches out of her way. Unseen things scratched her skin, and her arm was still throbbing. They hadn't gone far when a man stepped out in front of them. There was no emotion on his face as he aimed his weapon at them.

She didn't stop to think. "Go!" she yelled at the

others. She launched herself at the man.

He wasn't expecting her attack. Dani slammed into him and they fell in a tangle of arms and legs, his gun flying out of his hand.

She fought him. Hard. But he was strong and well-trained. When he shoved his hand against her gunshot wound, she screamed. Pain slashed through her with vicious claws. She went limp.

He punched her in the face and everything went blurry. With a grunt, he stood, sank a hand into her hair, and started dragging her back toward camp.

Dani felt tears stream down her face. Tears of pain and failure.

But as long as the others got away, that was all that mattered.

As the pain ebbed a little, she tried to think about what she could do. She could trip him, then go for his eyes and throat, and hit him between the legs.

She could hear the voices of the other Silk Road people getting louder. She heard the woman's angry tone.

Dani exploded into action. She twisted, ignoring the sharp sting to her scalp. She punched the man between his legs, felt soft things smash against her knuckles.

He let her go instantly, doubling over with a strangled groan. She stood and slammed a knee into his face. As he fell, she turned and ran.

She had no idea where she was going, she just ran blindly. It was pitch black, but she just kept moving. She needed as much distance between her and Silk Road as possible.

The branches slapped at her face and a few times she slipped, but she didn't stop.

Suddenly, she slammed into something hard. Hands grabbed at her.

She tried to jerk herself backward, twisting sharply.

"Dani. It's me."

She went still, air heaving in and out of her lungs. She couldn't see a damn thing. "Cal?"

"Yes." He yanked her close and she found herself pressed against a firm, warm chest.

*Thank God.* With a small sound, she pressed herself as close as she could get. She needed skin. She needed the reassurance they were both okay. She tore at the top buttons of his shirt, and pressed her face to the base of his throat. His skin was warm against her cheek, and she breathed him in. She smelled the blood, smoke and sweat, but beneath it was the scent of Cal.

It calmed something inside her, and she felt the crazy edge of fear ease a little.

"Shh." He stroked her hair. "You're okay." Then he pulled back, and she could just see the flash of his face in the darkness. "We have to go. Those guys are still out there, and they're after us."

She nodded and realized he couldn't see her. "Okay."

As though his words had summoned them, a shout echoed nearby.

Cal took her hand and broke into a run.

Dani had no idea how he could see where he was going. She followed him, trying not to stumble, and kept a tight hold on his hand.

Her boot hit something large, and she tripped. She expected to hit the ground, but Cal caught her, dragging her against his chest.

But if she expected sympathy from him she was wrong. He didn't talk, just made sure she was upright again, grabbed her wrist and kept moving.

Seconds turned to minutes. Dani lost track of any sense of time. She thought of Dr. Oakley and the others, and prayed they'd gotten away safely. Poor Jean-Luc. Her stomach did a slow, sickening roll. They'd shot him without blinking an eye. How could a single artifact, no matter its value, be worth somebody's life?

Suddenly, Cal stopped. Dani slammed into the back of him. He spun, pressing a finger to her lips.

Dread was like a rock in her belly. She strained to hear whatever it was that had caught his attention.

*Nothing.* Just the wind in the trees, and not even any of the regular jungle sounds. It seemed like even the animals were being quiet.

Then she heard it…voices.

She swallowed and looked up at Cal. He took her hand, changed direction, and pulled her back into the dense vegetation.

They were lost. She knew it. They had no map, no GPS. They were running deep into the middle of the jungle on a mountain in a remote corner of Cambodia. There was no Search and Rescue team to find them. What the hell were they going to do?

Cal stopped again. They were both breathing heavily, and now Dani could just make out a dirt path twisting off into the trees. She glanced up and realized the sky was starting to lighten. That, and the path, would make it easier going for them.

Then Cal turned away from the path and pulled her into the vegetation again.

"The path will be faster," she whispered. A vine slapped her in the face and she batted it away.

"They'll expect us to go that way. It'll be easier for them to track us."

*Right.* She concentrated on following close behind him and staying on her feet. Large tree roots protruded from the ground, but she managed to avoid them all. They hurried on and rounded a tree with a huge trunk.

Suddenly, Cal pitched forward. Dani felt the ground turn soggy beneath her feet. She sank up to her knees in mud and swallowed a small shriek.

Cal was letting out a stream of curses. He pulled one boot free of the mud.

*Damn.* Dani fought to pull her boots out of the sticky stuff, but it tried to suck her back down.

"Don't fight it," he warned. "We'll just end up sinking farther. Just go slowly."

She copied Cal's steady movements and slowly worked a foot free. By the time she was working to free her second leg, Cal was already free of the mud. He stood beside her, keeping a hold of her arm.

Dani tugged and tugged her leg, then hissed out

a short breath. "I'm stuck. My boot won't move."

"I've got you." Cal wrapped his arms around her chest, and gave a hard yank.

Her foot came free with a squelch and the momentum slammed her against Cal. They both toppled to the leafy ground.

He kept his arms around her, his face pressed to her hair. "Okay?"

She let her forehead drop against his chest for a minute. "I will be."

He slid a hand up and down her back. "Hell of a night."

She managed to mostly stifle a hysterical laugh. "You could say that."

He sat up, bringing her with him. "We haven't put enough distance between them and us. We need to keep moving."

Dani stood, grimacing at the mud coating her trousers and boots. There were several streaks on her shirt, but luckily none on her camera. She'd gotten pretty good at making sure her camera was protected whenever she fell or got mucky. It was second nature to her now.

"I don't understand any of this," she said. "We told them what we know. Nobody on Earth knows where the cintamani is."

"Silk Road are well-funded criminals...they don't care about lives. It was exactly the same when my brother came up against them in Egypt." Cal's tone was hard and grim. "They've been working behind the scenes for a long time, but it looks like they're stepping up their game. These guys that attacked us...they'll take whatever risk they need to on the small chance that they might stumble onto priceless treasure."

As they pushed through the undergrowth, Dani decided the jungle was even denser here. Vines, leaves, branches—everything seemed to have thorns that snagged on her clothes.

When they came out into a small clearing, it was almost a shock. The light was still murky, but it was enough to see a fallen tree on the ground. The large trunk was hollowed out and clearly used by the jungle animals for shelter.

Abruptly, Cal cursed. "I can hear them coming."

She sucked in a sharp breath. "We could hide." She eyed the trunk again.

Cal was scowling. "It's not a bad idea."

"The fallen tree—"

"Not there." He scanned around. "Over there." He moved over to a tree that looked like all the other trees around them. He pointed upward. "Get climbing."

"We're going to climb a tree?"

"Hurry. No questions."

Dragging in a deep breath, Dani eyed the tree. Then she gripped the trunk, and with a boost from Cal, started climbing. When she reached the lowest branches, she grabbed on and pulled herself up.

It was tricky, and a few times her boots slid off the branches. She added a few new scratches to her injuries, and the wound on her arm was burning, but finally she pulled herself up onto a thicker branch.

Cal moved up beside her. "Higher."

Dani rolled her eyes but didn't protest. Finally, they settled onto a larger, higher branch. The foliage closed in around them. She shivered, more conscious now of the cooler morning air on her bare skin. An arm wrapped around her, pulling her into the warmth of Cal's body.

"What now?" she whispered.

"We wait."

Dani had never minded waiting before. Waiting for the perfect shot, the perfect light, or the perfect expression on someone's face was easy for her. But sitting damp, scared, and tired—not to mention in pain—in the top of a tree in the middle of the jungle, was definitely much more difficult.

She shifted, and pain shot through her arm. She tried to stay quiet but Cal picked up on it instantly.

"What's wrong? You've been outstanding, Dani. Just hang in there a bit longer."

She nodded. "But I got shot, though. It really hurts."

"Let me take a look." He pulled her hand away from her arm, probing at her wound. The breath hissed out of him.

Her stomach clenched. "Oh, God. How bad is it?"

"Well...it'll need a Band-Aid."

Dani heard the amusement in his tone and stiffened. "A Band-Aid? It hurts more than a damn Band-Aid."

"Dani, the bullet only grazed you." He brushed her hair off her face. "You're fine."

Her hair was hopelessly tangled. "I look like

crap and I've been shot…that's not fine."

The tiniest smile tweaked his lips. "Well, crap looks good on you."

"Liar."

"And you weren't shot, you were grazed. You've got a small graze there, that's it."

"Quit rubbing it in," she grumbled.

He cupped her jaw and suddenly his face turned serious. "When I saw you get hit…I was…" His voice broke off.

Something softened inside her and she pressed a hand over his on her cheek. "I'm fine, Cal. I was far more worried about you, afraid they'd kill you."

They stared at each other for a moment and Dani felt her mouth go dry. She realized just how much her admission revealed about her feelings for this man. God, she couldn't really be falling for him in the middle of this hellish mess, could she?

She cleared her throat. "Do you think Jean-Luc and the others are okay?"

Cal pulled in a deep breath. "I hope so. Silk Road seemed focused on you and me. If they can get out of here, and get Jean-Luc to a doctor, he'll be fine."

Then Cal straightened, and tapped her shoulder before pressing a finger to his mouth. She went as stiff as a board and peered down through the branches at the small clearing below. She couldn't see anything.

Cal moved just his finger to point off to the left. That's when she saw the shadows creeping along at the edge of the tree line. There were three of them, all dressed in black, moving silently through the vegetation.

As the men got closer, she heard them murmuring amongst themselves. There was enough light now to make out the guns in their hands.

It only took them seconds to move over to the hollow log and look inside. Dani closed her eyes and thanked God Cal had vetoed her dumb idea.

The Silk Road men did another loop of the clearing before melting away into the trees again.

Cal moved a little and she felt his lips press against her ear. "We need to stay here a bit longer. Make sure they're really gone."

She managed to nod, hunching her shoulders.

"Why don't you get some sleep?" he suggested.

"Sleep?" she whispered. "After all this, you think I'll be able to sleep? In a tree?"

She saw the flash of his white teeth. "I won't let you fall."

No, he wouldn't. She knew that deep in her marrow. She knew Cal would give his life to take care of others, to take care of her.

Dani snuggled closer to the safe hardness of him. She was sure that there was no way that she would fall asleep.

But exhaustion and the dying adrenaline rush proved too much for her. Her eyelids grew heavy, and when Cal tucked her face in under his chin, the steady beat of his heart under her ear soothed her.

Sleep dragged her under.

# Chapter Nine

Despite their situation, Cal was enjoying holding Dani in his arms. He sensed when she finally drifted off, trusting him to look out for her. He stroked a hand against her hair, watching the steady rise and fall of her chest.

She'd done damn well in the insanity. She hadn't fallen apart. She'd fought back.

That horrible moment when he'd seen her get shot... He squeezed his eyes closed. He saw Marty's bloody face as Cal held him in his arms. The SEAL, the *friend*, whose back he'd always vowed to watch out for.

The friend who'd died in his arms.

For a second, the thick, jungle trees around him dissolved into memory, and he heard the rat-a-tat of automatic gunfire, felt the desert sun on his face, heard the frantic shouts. Felt the sticky slide of Marty's blood on his hands.

Cal's hold tightened on Dani, and she made a small sound and moved her face against his chest, burrowing deeper. Cal released a shaky breath. She was alive. She was okay.

He needed to get her out of the jungle and back to safety. He wished like hell he still had his satellite phone. Still, when he didn't check in with Darcy, she'd know something was up. All Treasure Hunter Security team members had a tracking device buried in their watches. It would lead the guys straight through to them.

But it would take a long time for Logan and Morgan to reach them. Too long.

He stroked her hair again. Fucking Silk Road. For so long they'd been just shadows, only vague rumors, whispered about in dark corners. There'd been digs where artifacts had gone quietly missing, and artifacts that had mysteriously walked out of museum exhibitions. People had really known nothing about Silk Road.

Well, it looked like they were out now—loud and proud.

Cal turned his wrist over without waking Dani and looked at his watch. The sun was rising, and they wouldn't have the cover of darkness to help them evade their pursuers. Best case, the bastards would go and leave them alone now that they knew they didn't have the cintamani.

But Cal's gut told him there was no way that was going to happen. They didn't want to leave witnesses.

Logan and Morgan would come. For now, Cal and Dani just had to stay hidden and hold on until then.

When the temperature rose and more sunlight filtered through the trees, he shook Dani awake. "Time to go, beautiful."

She blinked sleepily. She looked damn sweet,

with her flushed cheeks and sleep still sliding out of her eyes. That prickly exterior of hers was down. Her hair was a mass of dark tangles around her face, and she had a streak of mud on her cheek. Cal wondered why he found her more beautiful than ever before.

He reached out and started gently untangling her hair.

She was watching him. "We can't stay here?"

"It's safer if we keep moving. All we have to do is put some distance between us and Silk Road, and hold on until my team gets here. I thought we'd find a safe place to clean up and rest."

She gave a small nod. "How will your team find us?"

He lifted his wrist. "Tracker in my watch. If anything happens to me, you take this with you."

Her face paled a little. "I'd prefer if nothing happened to you. You promised me a comfy hotel bed with fresh sheets."

He reached out and touched her chin, gently stroking her jawline. "So I did. I've got lots of things I want to do to you." He dragged his thumb over her lips. "Naughty, dirty things."

She watched him steadily. "Oh?"

"And after those things…" After a job, Cal liked to head into the mountains and go climbing or skiing. For some reason, he couldn't imagine leaving Dani alone in a bed to rush off and do that. "Well, let's just say I'm planning to not step foot in the jungle for a really long time."

She laughed. "I hear you."

They shimmied down the tree and Cal swung his pack on his back. The light weight of it made him frown. He was very aware they had limited supplies and food.

*One thing at a time, Ward.* He nudged Dani ahead of him and they set off into the trees.

It was easier going in the daylight. Cal watched and listened for any sign of Silk Road. Nothing.

"I'd really like to wash this mud off." Dani was looking down at her boots and legs. She was caked with mud and Cal's clothes hadn't fared much better. "Do you think they're gone?"

He knew who she was talking about. "No. Silk Road is stubborn. They've set their sights on the cintamani, and they'll keep looking until they find it. Rumor is that the Silk Road bosses don't tolerate failure."

Dani shivered. "And who are the Silk Road bosses?"

"No one knows."

"Well, I'll be happy to never set eyes on anyone from Silk Road again."

After a few hours, Cal fished nutrition bars from the backpack and made her eat. The deeper they went into the jungle, the hotter it got and more mosquitos buzzed around. Soon, Cal felt perspiration gathering on his forehead and soaking the back of his shirt. At least there hadn't been any sign that Silk Road was following them.

"What's that?"

Dani's sharp voice made him turn. She was pointing off to the right through the trees.

He pushed ahead of her and could just make out a flash of white against the vibrant green. He pulled his SIG out. "Stay behind me."

They moved cautiously through the trees. Cal pushed back some vines and his eyes widened.

Then he heard a *click*.

Dani moved past him, her camera held up. "Oh my God, it's amazing."

Nestled amongst the trees, tangled with vines, was the wreck of a plane.

By the look of it, it had crashed a long time ago. The main part of the fuselage was still intact, but the tail was long gone and the wings had been shattered. The jungle was doing its best to claim it back. Trees, shrubs and vines were growing through the broken windows and the large hole torn in the side.

"It looks like an old transport." It was too damaged for him to tell the make and model. "Looks pretty old, though."

Dani made a small noise but was already absorbed with taking her photos. Cal shook his head. God forbid anyone get between Dani and her shot.

After she was finished, Cal carefully climbed inside. It looked like it had been picked over a long time ago, but he took a quick look around. There might be something they could use.

He found a blanket still in a plastic wrap folded under a seat. It wasn't much but it would do. He tucked it into his backpack.

"Let's keep moving," he said.

She gave the plane one last wistful glance and they moved off. He could see the tiredness etched on her face. They needed to rest soon.

Cal tried to judge their location and arc of the sun, and circle them back to head in the direction of the closest village, but the trees made it damn hard to stay on track.

But as long as they were nowhere near Silk Road, he was happy.

Not long later, Cal heard a faint noise and stopped.

Dani tensed. "Is it them?"

He ran a hand down her arm. "Nope." He smiled. "It's something else. Follow me."

He moved a little quicker now, and a moment later they broke out of the trees. A shallow river lay ahead of them, and just beyond a small bend, Cal heard the soothing rush of a waterfall.

Dani's brow furrowed. "Is that...?" A smile broke out on her face and she pushed ahead of him at a jog.

Cal followed, and as they rounded the bend, he saw a pretty little waterfall tumbling over some rocks. It wasn't very high, maybe as tall as he was, but it was glorious fresh water.

The huge smile on Dani's face made him feel like a hero. She glanced up at him. "Is it safe enough to wash?"

The river wasn't very deep, and after a quick look around, he nodded. "Go for it."

She gave a long groan. "I can't wait to get clean." She set her camera down and then pulled her tank over her head, leaving her in a simple, black bra.

Cal cleared his throat. "Go wash. I'll do a quick sweep of the perimeter." No one was getting close to Dani.

She grinned at him over her bare shoulder. "Thank you."

With a nod, he headed back into the trees. He was not going to think about her stripping those clothes off. Of her in the water naked, water slicking over her smooth skin.

"Fuck." His cock went hard.

He huffed out a breath. She'd had a rough night. He wasn't going to take advantage of her. Once they were out of here, though…well, then all bets were off. But right now, he was going to pull himself together and not be an asshole.

Cal forced himself to walk the perimeter. He saw no signs that anyone was near them. No sounds, no distant voices. They'd put some distance between them and Silk Road, enough that they could rest a little, but he wouldn't be completely happy until he had Dani out of the jungle.

He found a spot, hidden by denser vegetation, on slightly higher ground. He spread out the blanket and set his backpack down. It was the safest spot.

Dani should've had enough time to wash and get clean by now. He headed back toward the waterfall. He stepped out of the trees and froze.

The air lodged in his chest and his blood started pounding. A raw, primal beat.

She was completely naked under the water, her face lifted up to the spray. She'd washed her clothes, and they were neatly laid out on a rock nearby.

But Cal couldn't drag his eyes away from her.

She was long, with gentle curves and slim, toned legs. Her hair was slick—a mass of dark, wet curls down her back.

Need slammed into him. He couldn't ever remember wanting with an urgency and a hunger like this.

\*\*\*

Dani washed away the horror and tiredness of the night.

The cool water felt wonderful on her skin, slicking away the dirt, mud, and blood. She lost track of how long she'd stood there, the water pounding over her head.

Then she felt two strong arms wrap around her from behind, and she gasped.

She didn't have time to be afraid. She recognized him in an instant—his lean, dependable strength, and the warm scent of him.

His lips pressed against the side of her neck and she arched back into him. In a second, her body went from cool to molten. Desire flared like a spark hitting gasoline.

She spun and pressed her mouth to his. She heard a greedy, feral sound and realized it had come from her. She'd spent so long being afraid of her desire and now, it seemed this man had thrown the floodgates wide open.

He kissed her hard, his tongue sliding into her mouth to tease and taste. Her hands dug into his shoulders, kneading the hard muscles. She felt ridges under her fingertips—scars, she realized. Later she promised to take the time to explore them.

But right now she needed more. So much more. She felt reckless, out-of-control and she loved it. His kiss took on a hard, savage edge.

Then he tore his mouth from hers, setting her back a bit.

She glanced up, seeing the desire on his face, and the visible control he was exerting.

His hands fisted. "Dani. You've had a rough night. You've been shot—"

"Grazed."

He raised a brow. "Oh, so now it's a graze?" He shook his head and blew out a breath. "Your defenses are down, Dani. I won't take advantage of you."

She watched him back up a step. She spotted his gun resting on a rock nearby and he'd taken his shirt off—holy hell, that chest of his was biteable—but had left his trousers on. His cock was a hard, thick outline against the dark fabric.

He took another step back and her chest tightened. Callum Ward, the man who'd told her he was all about a hot, temporary good time was acting unbelievably thoughtful and noble. She felt his need throbbing off him.

She stepped up to him and stopped, only an inch between them. "Cal, I'm fine."

ANNA HACKETT

He shook his head.

"I'm alive. Thanks to you. We made it out of there alive, and I'm damn happy about that." She reached up and cupped her breasts.

His hot gaze zeroed in there. Torment lined his face. "God, you are so beautiful. Long and lean, those pretty breasts topped by those pretty pink nipples."

Heat pooled between her legs. "You promised me naughty, dirty things."

He shuddered. "I don't take advantage...I don't want you to hate me after."

Like that could ever happen. Dani was always honest with herself. "Shut up, Cal."

She wasn't sure who reached first, but the next thing she knew, they were both grabbing each other.

His mouth found hers. The wild, savage kiss stole her breath and made her pulse leap. His hands ran up her sides

"So smooth." His voice was gravelly, husky. He cupped her breasts, his fingers flicking across her nipples.

Dani gripped him, scraping her nails up his chest and across his broad shoulders. He spun them both, and the water poured over them. He bent her back, his mouth latching onto her nipple. She cried out, the sound swallowed by the water, and sank her hands into his hair.

As he moved to the other breast, she reached down blindly, yanking at the buttons on his trousers.

He groaned against her skin. "I feel like I've wanted you forever."

"Me too."

He looked up, smiling. "Since you were rude to me at Angkor."

"So cocky."

He thrust his hips forward. "Absolutely."

She laughed and he started backing her up. When her back hit warm rock, she leaned forward and pressed her lips to his chest. She rained kisses across the skin, still tugging at his waistband. Finally, she got his trousers open. Cal kicked free of them and his boxers, nabbed the garments, and tossed them onto the riverbank.

A second later, Dani cupped his cock in her hands.

"Hell." He grabbed her and pressed her against the rock. She made a small needy sound in her throat and he kissed her again. They grabbed at each other with greedy hands. Cal's hand slipped between her thighs and she arched into him.

"So soft, beautiful, and so very wet."

"Yes, just there," she panted. "Don't stop, Cal."

"You like that?" He dragged his fingers across her flesh, before sinking one thick finger inside her. He moved his thumb in a slippery circle, centering his caress on her clit.

She jerked against him. "Yes."

He kept working her, and her body trembled, one big mass of need.

Then he pulled his hand away.

She gasped. "No—"

His hands slid beneath her ass and he boosted her up. She wrapped her legs around his lean hips, and when his cock brushed against her, they both groaned. He moved his hips and she felt the thick head of his cock lodge between her lips.

Then he stilled, his muscles straining under her hands. "Shit...I don't have a condom."

"I'm healthy," she panted. "And I have a contraceptive implant."

He grabbed her thighs, pushing them wide. "I'm clean. And I haven't had unprotected sex since...hell, I never have."

She licked her lips and saw the hot, possessive flare in his eyes. "I want you inside me."

With one hard thrust, he lodged himself inside her.

***

"Cal!"

Yeah, it felt good. Sensation crashed over Cal, along with Dani's half sobs. He held himself deep inside her, memorizing the feel of her and fighting off the wicked, edgy need to mate. She was so hot and tight around him. Want clawed at his gut.

Her nails bit into his shoulders. "Move, damn you."

Her words snapped his control, setting his savage need free. He pulled out, then slammed back inside her. With hard thrusts, he drove himself inside her. She made a guttural sound, and Cal grabbed her hands, threading their fingers together and pinned them above her head.

As his hips pistoned, his vision narrowed to just her face. The glint of her different colored eyes, the angles of her face and those full lips. It was a face that shouldn't have been so beautiful, but to him, it felt like his everything.

Cal felt her body shuddering and knew she was getting close. He kept moving thickly inside her, shocked at this craving he had for her. For him, sex had always been a quick, easy ride, not this all-consuming passion.

"I'm going to come," she cried.

Flesh slapped against flesh. "Come, Dani. But you have to be quiet, baby. One day, I'll make you scream my name as loud as you can...but for now, kiss me and come on my cock."

She looked up, shocked pleasure crossing her face. Her eyelids fluttered closed as her release crashed over her. Her hips surged forward, her mouth met his and Cal swallowed her scream.

A second later, he slammed inside her and held himself there, stretching her wide. He groaned as he came inside her.

They stayed there, just his weight holding them against the rock. Hell, Cal wasn't sure he could move, but he was more than happy to stay like this, pressed against Dani's slim body. He turned his head, burying his face in her hair.

She moved and her inner muscles gripped him.

He gave a tortured groan. "No more, woman, you've wrecked me."

She turned her face against his cheek and

smiled. "Is that a complaint?"

"Hell, no. I plan to do a lot more to you, and let you wreck me some more." With another groan, he pulled away from the wall, carrying her against him.

He snatched up his SIG and their clothes, and made it back to the riverbank. He carried her to the safer spot he'd found earlier. He knelt and laid her on the blanket. Now there was a pretty sight. He'd had those long, slender legs clamped around his hips mere moments ago, and damned if he didn't want them there again. He planted one knee between her legs and leaned over her.

"I could look at you all day."

She shifted, her smile lazy and satisfied. "You're only going to look?"

"Well...I am thinking of making love to you again." He leaned down and pressed a kiss to her belly. She quivered under his lips. "It was pretty damned great the first time."

"It was." Her hands slid into his hair.

He kissed her all over, trailing kisses over her breasts. He paused to press a kiss at the graze on her arm.

"Scared the hell out of me when I saw you get shot," he said again.

She shifted her hands to cup his cheeks, her eyes turning serious. "I'm fine. Lucky for me, you're very good at your job."

He pulled in a deep breath. "I try my damnedest. People's lives depend on it." He felt the ripple of old pain. "I've failed before."

She forced his gaze back to hers. "No one's perfect, Cal. And believe me, what you do…I don't know anyone who'd risk themselves to protect someone else. None of the people in my life would ever put someone else before themselves." Her fingers stroked his cheeks. "You're a hero."

"Shut up."

"Oh, you don't like hearing you're a hero?"

He moved down and nipped her belly. He grazed his teeth over her hip bone.

She arched up. "You're trying to distract me."

"Is it working?" He made a growling sound and nipped at her inner thigh. "Maybe I'll have to find another way to keep you quiet. And unfortunately, we do need to be quiet. We're hidden here, but I'm not taking any chances."

When his mouth moved between her legs, and closed over her, her hips reared up and she cried out. "No, Cal."

He gave her another lick. "You don't like this?"

"I've never really enjoyed it. I don't like feeling like I'm under a damn spotlight." A flash of vulnerability crossed her face. "I'd prefer to have you in my mouth."

Damn, the image of her lips stretched around his cock made his blood pound. But he knew what was going on. His beautiful lover didn't like giving up control. He kissed her thigh again. "Baby, I am so going to give you the chance. But right now, I want you to lie back and enjoy."

She flopped back on the blanket, her body as stiff as a board.

"There's no rush, we have all the time in the world." He kept his voice low and lazy. "I could just sit here looking at you, right here in this private place where you're all pink and wet and swollen from having me inside you."

She writhed against the blanket.

"Just let go. Enjoy." He pressed his mouth to her, with no intention of being gentle.

He sucked and licked at her, loving her taste. Again, her hands tangled in his hair, tugging hard.

"Too…much," she panted, twisting beneath him.

Then he sealed his lips over her clit and sucked.

Dani's body went taut and she made a restrained, incoherent sound. Cal's cock was hard again, need biting into him. He lowered his body on top of hers and pushed her thighs out wide. When he slid his cock inside, it felt like coming home.

This time, his thrusts were slower. He didn't feel that urgent rush like the first time. He took his time and when she peaked again, he was with her, groaning his release as she sank her teeth into his shoulder to muffle her cries.

Emptied out, feeling damn good, he dropped down beside her and pulled her into the curve of his body.

"Thank you," she murmured.

He nuzzled the sensitive spot under her ear. "Beautiful, if I accept that, I'd be an asshole, since I got just as much out of that as you did." He kissed the side of her neck. "But, you know, if you're in a giving mood, I have a few ideas."

Her slap to his chest had a fair bit of sting to it.

# Chapter Ten

Dani dozed, the warmth of the jungle and Cal's hard body keeping her wrapped in a secure cocoon. Her body had several delicious aches and she didn't even mind that Cal had spritzed them both with mosquito repellant.

She was conscious of the fact that Cal didn't fall into a deep sleep, but was still somehow alert and aware. His gun lay just inches away. She turned to look at him. His face was more relaxed and had lost some of that rough edge, despite his sexy scruff.

His body was still hard and tough. As she took in the scars across his chest, her belly clenched. He'd been hurt before. She reached out and touched one thick ridge of scar across his belly. He'd fought for his country and been injured doing it.

She leaned down and peppered kisses across the scars. She really liked the way this man was built—hard muscles, bronze skin. He made a deep sound in his throat that said he was enjoying her exploration.

Dani pushed him onto his back and swung her leg over his hips, straddling him. She leaned down and kept kissing his chest, taking her time to lick his nipples.

When she raised her head, he was watching her, his blue eyes burning.

"Well, this is a much better way to wake up." In one smooth move, he sat up, his hands clenching her butt.

She kissed him. It started out lazy, a sexy exploration, but desire ignited. He groaned, his tongue slipping into her mouth, and she kissed him back with all the hunger growing in her belly.

He tugged her hair back, attacking her throat. "God, Dani, you are so sexy."

She felt his cock beneath her, hard and ready. She lifted her hips, gripped him and lined him up. Then she sank down.

He groaned. She rose and fell on him, slowly at first, working him in and out. God, he stretched her, filled her. She saw he was looking down, watching where they were joined and it made her muscles clench.

His strong fingers bit into her skin, urging her to move faster. Then he was slamming her down and Dani let her head drop back. As she came, a cry ripped from her throat and she jammed her fist against her mouth to stifle it.

"Dammit...Dani." He pulled her down hard and held her there, emptying himself inside her.

She collapsed against his chest, her head on his shoulder, and tried to catch her breath. Her entire body was vibrating.

A hand stroked down her back. "Sorry I couldn't give you that comfy bed. I'd like to be ordering you room service about now." After another kiss, he set her back on the blanket and reached for his backpack.

Dani watched the interesting flex of muscles in his tight butt and thighs. Damn, the man should not wear clothes...ever. She pulled her camera closer, itching to take a shot of him. But she wouldn't, not without his permission.

"I'd love a shot of you like this."

He stiffened like he'd touched a live wire. "Naked?"

"Nude." God, the discomfort on his face was cute. "Laid out on the blanket, a big, healthy male animal." She could picture it clearly.

"I'm not posing for porn."

"Porn!" She sniffed. "I am an artist. It wouldn't be porn." Her gaze ran over him. Oh yes, she could capture that bronze skin, the defined muscles and ridges. "It would only be for me."

"Says every person who ever convinced someone to pose nude before they uploaded it to the Internet."

"Chicken." She vowed she would get that shot, one day.

He handed her another nutrition bar and grinned. "Well, you're naked, too. I'll let you take a nude shot of me, if I can do the same to you."

Dani grabbed her now-clean panties and tank from the tangled pile of clothes. "No. I'm the photographer, not the subject." She heard him chuckling and ignored him. Her trousers weren't quite dry, so she'd left them on a branch. Cal, completely unconcerned about being naked, didn't bother covering up. She wasn't complaining. Plus, she liked the fact that he trusted her enough not to sneak a shot of him.

She munched on her granola bar and turned on her camera. She started flicking through her images. When she saw one of Jean-Luc and Sakada smiling for the camera, her throat tightened. "God, I hope the others made it out."

"Me too."

Another image showed the intricate details of one of the temple walls. "Do you think the cintamani is really out here somewhere?"

Cal shrugged. "Maybe. Pretty sure Silk Road will leave no stone unturned to try and find it."

And hurt a lot of people in the process.

She looked at the image of the temple wall again. She saw the people who had made the temple had captured its design on the wall. She could clearly make out the pyramid shape, and the image of the cintamani stone was etched above it. Two carved grooves ran from the temple—one up and one to the right.

She leaned down, bringing up the next wall of the temple. This one showed a single tower, with the cintamani again etched above it. Dancing women, gods and goddesses, were carved into the wall around it. Again, she saw those interesting grooves radiating out from the cintamani—this time heading down and to the right.

She set her half-eaten granola bar down and flicked to the next image.

"You ever just stop and enjoy the moment?"

She looked up. Cal was drinking some water from his bottle. She snagged it and took a long sip. "Uh huh." She took her time, dragging her lips slowly off the end of the bottle.

He shook his head with a grin. "Tease."

She closed her eyes for a second, moaning a little.

"Knock it off, Navarro. How are your photos looking?"

She straightened with a smile. "I'm pretty happy with them. Once we make it back to civilization…" Hell, *if* they made it out of here. No, she couldn't think like that. Cal said his team would come, and she trusted him. Funny, that she trusted this man—a man who'd been a stranger and one she'd initially disliked—more than anyone else. "Once I can get my laptop, I'll do a little bit of editing to them. Make them shine."

She turned the camera so he could see the screen.

"Wow. Amazing."

His praise made her glow inside. It was of the elephant at Srah Damrei. She'd captured the jungle light and shadow just right, and it looked like the giant elephant was alive, and about to walk away. She pressed the button. Her next shot showed Dr. Oakley inside the linga temple, a hand touching the engraved wall, his face focused. The next was a haunting image of the linga temple from the outside, nestled in the jungle, the green vegetation topping it like icing on a cake.

"You are damn good at your work, Dani."

She grinned at him. "Thank you." She kept the slideshow going.

Cal spotted a picture of himself and frowned. "That's not how I look."

"Heroic? Adventurous? It's exactly how you look."

He made an annoyed sound that made her hide her smile. The next shots showed the temple wall images she'd been looking at before.

"Your images from inside the temple are awesome." He dropped down beside her. "I'll remember that place fondly."

She slapped his arm. "Surely you can't be thinking of sex after what we did this morning."

"I can always think about sex." He reached out and toyed with the neckline of her tank, his fingers brushing at the skin between her breasts. "Especially if you're sitting half-naked beside me."

"Well, you're *completely* naked. Maybe you should put some clothes on?"

He grinned at her. "My naked body too distracting for you?"

She shot him a look. "I'm not deigning to answer that. Your ego is healthy enough as it is." But her gaze drifted downward and she rolled her eyes. "Oh, all right, you're gorgeous. Now get some clothes on."

He did pull his cargo trousers on, wincing a little. "Still damp." He didn't bother buttoning them.

"Damp but no longer coated in mud and blood."

"True."

She looked at her photos again. "I'm really happy I could capture the best moments of this trip...before everything went horribly wrong." The next image of the temple wall appeared. The center of this one showed some sort of small shrine, the oval cintamani above it. And those strange lines again, these ones heading up and to the left. "I think they really tell a story..."

Dani's mind whirled and she frowned. She tapped the camera buttons, looked at the fourth and final wall of the temple. She saw those grooves again. She pulled up the four images all at once. Damn, they were small on this screen, and she wished she had her laptop.

"What is it, Navarro?"

"I'm not sure...but the pictures on each of the four walls, when you arrange them like this—" She held the camera up. "They kind of fit together."

Cal's brow furrowed as he studied the images. "I see what you mean. Those grooves make a square with a temple or tower at each corner." He stiffened. "Shit. It isn't a square, it's a quincunx!"

Her eyes widened. "The design they used for all their temples. The square with—"

"Another point in the center. What was in the center of the temple, Dani?"

"This." She found the image. "A statue of a naga holding the linga, the cintamani."

Cal sat back on his heels. "The linga temple makes one corner of the quincunx..."

Excitement was a dizzying fizz in her blood. "And that tower we passed on the way must be this corner." She pointed at the image of the four walls again.

Cal moved his finger over her screen. "So the cintamani should be in the center."

Dani's head snapped up. "God, that Silk Road woman was right...there is a map to the stone."

\*\*\*

Cal stared down at Dani's photos. Damn, it all fit together. A map to the cintamani stone.

"My sense of direction is pretty good and I memorized a map of the area before we came to Phnom Kulen. I don't think we're too far from the center of the quincunx."

She scrambled to her knees. "We have to find the cintamani before Silk Road does, Cal."

"No."

She threw her hands out. "We're lost out here. Waiting for your team. We may as well follow these clues to the stone."

Cal stayed silent, a muscle in his jaw working. He didn't want Dani in this jungle, anywhere near Silk Road. "I want you safe."

She pressed her hands to his chest. "I'm safe with you. Come on, you want to find it." Her voice lowered. "Let's do it. For the team. For Jean-Luc."

Cal scowled.

"It was you who told me I needed to experience life. To truly live."

His scowl deepened. "I am aware of the fact that you are using your feminine wiles to wrap me around your little finger like a pretzel."

"Is it working?"

"Maybe." Heaven help him if she ever realized how much he'd do for her. He let out a breath. "Okay. We can *look*. But if we spot any evidence of Silk Road, we're going to hide and wait for my team."

"Deal." She was grinning at him. "For all your sexy, tough-guy looks, you're pretty easy."

He pulled her close and pressed a quick kiss to her lips. "I'll show you just how easy, if you're not careful."

Soon, they were dressed, and Cal had packed up their meager possessions. As they headed off into the jungle, the sound of the waterfall faded.

It wasn't long before they were both hot and sweaty again, their private dip a distant dream.

Cal wasn't convinced they were going to find anything. Rubble and ruins at best. Hell, he wasn't even sure he wanted to find this damn stone.

As they pushed through a particularly thick patch of jungle, Dani came to a stop with a huff. "Damn. We haven't seen a single stone or statue. Nothing to indicate humans were ever here."

"You didn't think it was going to be easy, did you?"

"No. But what if my theory isn't right? What if those lines on the wall were just that—lines?"

Cal opened his backpack and handed her the bottle of water. "What's your gut tell you?"

"I don't listen to my gut. I trust facts."

"Bullshit. Every time you lift that camera, you're

using your instincts. What do they tell you?"

She lifted her chin. "I'm not wrong."

"You didn't imagine what you saw on the walls. I didn't notice until you pointed it out. You found the pattern. The map is real."

Her gaze traced his face, and then she lifted her camera and snapped a shot of him. "You should stop saying and doing things that make me like you more, Cal Ward." She glanced away. "I might not want to let you go after this."

Cal felt a tangle of emotions rise in him. Desire, satisfaction, and if he was honest, a tiny thread of fear. He knew he'd never wanted a woman like he wanted Dani, and it scared the hell out of him. What if he messed up? What if he hurt her?

"Dani?"

She lifted her face, and there was a soft look in her eyes. He lifted a hand—

But then her face changed. Her gaze moved past his shoulder and the soft look turned to horror.

Cal was already turning, but it was too late.

Something slammed into his head. Cal sprawled forward on the ground. He was reaching for his SIG, fighting to stay conscious. He saw Dani scramble to her feet and launch herself forward.

Something smashed into his head again, and this time, everything went black.

\*\*\*

Cal groaned, blinking his eyes. He could taste dirt in his mouth. What the hell?

His head was throbbing and he was trying to work out where the hell he was.

Cal raised his head and saw jungle.

He pushed himself up to a sitting position, groaning as his head gave another vicious throb. He touched the back of his head and felt a lump and the damp stickiness of blood. Then fear shot through him.

*Dani.*

He scrambled to his feet and turned. He ignored his headache, ignored everything, searching for a sign of her.

*Nothing.* Then he spotted something on the ground.

Her camera.

His heart clenched. He picked it up and slipped the strap over his head. He crouched and looked at the scuff marks on the ground. Someone with a size thirteen boot had been here. Whoever it was that had hit Cal hard.

And whoever it was now had Dani.

Cal's jaw locked. He knew it had to be Silk Road. He touched his side and realized his gun was gone. He didn't care. Weapon or no weapon, he was going after his woman. *Hold on, beautiful.*

# Chapter Eleven

Dani tried her hardest to drag her feet and trip over something, anything to slow them down.

Her captor gave her another hard prod in the back. "Keep moving."

Cal would come.

If Cal was okay.

She tasted bile in her mouth. The Silk Road bastard had hit Cal hard. Seeing him unconscious, sprawled on the ground... God.

Ahead, she heard people talking. Her captor shoved her again, and she stumbled forward into a small clearing. People turned to look at her.

She scanned them and let out a breath. She didn't see Dr. Oakley, or any of the others on their team. They must have gotten away safely.

"Welcome back." The Silk Road woman stepped forward, her gaze frosty. "I didn't get a chance to introduce myself. I'm Raven."

Dani stayed silent. All she could think about was Cal lying motionless in the dirt, blood running from the back of his head.

"Where is the cintamani?" Raven asked.

Dani purposely looked to the woman's left and into the trees.

Raven circled Dani. "In my...previous employment, my job was getting people to talk." The woman's smile looked pleasant, like she was chatting to a friend. "Particularly when they didn't want to."

"I've got nothing to tell you. I'm not an archeologist, I'm a photographer. I was on this expedition to capture the journey. I don't know anything about Cambodian history or this fucking stupid stone."

Raven tilted her head. "A photographer?"

"That's right."

"That makes you Daniela Navarro." The woman looked at the men gathered nearby. "Confirm her identity." She looked back at Dani. "And you know nothing of the stone, Ms. Navarro?"

"Yes."

Raven reached out, her fingers brushing over Dani's cheek. Dani fought not to jerk away.

"I'm very good at reading the minutest of body language." She slapped Dani on the cheek, hard. The blow was enough to knock Dani onto her hands and knees.

Dani shook her head, trying to ignore the sting.

"Where is the cintamani stone?" the woman asked again.

"Fuck you."

This time Dani felt the cool brush of metal at her temple. Her muscles locked, and her stomach felt like a rock.

"I would prefer not to have to shoot you," Raven said.

Dani closed her eyes. Her thoughts turned to Cal. For the first time in her life, she wanted to be with someone. She wanted to share her life with somebody else. She wanted to let the scary, bright feelings in her loose and love Cal Ward.

"Last time. Where is the cintamani stone?"

Dani held onto those thoughts of Cal.

Raven sighed. "Okay, Ms. Navarro. Brock and Casper, find Callum Ward...and kill him."

Dani's head snapped up.

Satisfaction crossed Raven's face. "Ah, now I have your attention. I'll tell them to stop, if you tell me what you know."

Dani gnawed on her lip.

"Last I heard, Ward was facedown and out cold. It'll be simple for my men to put a bullet in his brain."

No one else was going to die for this damn stone. Dani closed her eyes in defeat. "There is a map. It's on the walls of the Temple of the Sacred Linga. I took pictures of it and worked out how it fit them together."

"I knew it." Raven smiled. "I need the images."

Dani felt the urge to smile. "They're on my camera."

The woman raised a brow then looked at the man who'd captured Dani. "You left her camera behind?"

If the situation wasn't so dire, Dani would've laughed. The man looked supremely uncomfortable. "Sorry. Didn't think it was important—"

160

"Idiot." Raven glanced at another man. "Khan, you took shots inside the linga temple, right?"

The man nodded. "Yeah."

"Bring me the camera." The woman held out her hand.

The man brought a camera over. It wasn't as large or as good quality as Dani's, but it was decent. The woman turned it over and started flicking through the photos.

The man shifted. "I didn't get everything. There wasn't time."

Dani arched her head to catch a glimpse of the images. They weren't as good as hers, but dammit. It looked like there were enough.

"I think we have most of the images." The woman's dark eyes bored into Dani. "Tell me how they go together."

Something inside Dani trembled for a second. She didn't want these bastards to have the cintamani…but it wasn't worth Cal's life. And hell, the damn thing might not even be there.

"The images on the four walls go together to form a quincunx." Dani picked up a stick off the ground and started drawing the shape in the dirt. Then she pointed at one corner. "I believe the linga temple is this corner."

The woman nodded. "And where is the cintamani?"

"I'm not really sure. I can't translate the text and…"

"Speculate, Ms. Navarro. I'm guessing that's what you and Mr. Ward were doing."

Dani hedged a little. "Maybe one of the other corners..."

Raven made a sound. "Nice try." She turned to her men. "The cintamani would be in the center of the square. We still need to know one of the other corners." She looked back at Dani.

Dani schooled her face to be blank. They didn't know the tower was one of the other corners. "I can't help you there. That's as far as we'd gotten."

Raven's gaze was intense, like a spotlight. She scrutinized every inch of Dani's face before turning away. "Kahn, you're the archeologist. Work it out."

The man swallowed. "I'll do my—"

"Just do it, Kahn."

The man spent some time hunched over a tablet. Suddenly, he sat up straight. "Raven...this tower...it looks like the one we passed on our way to the linga temple."

Dani felt her heart drop.

Then she realized Raven was watching her. The woman's mouth moved into an icy smile. "That's it, Khan. Ms. Navarro's dismay just confirmed it."

Soon she found herself trudging through the jungle again, flanked by two of the Silk Road men.

They walked for what felt like hours. It was hot and steamy, and Dani was parched, but no one had given her any water.

"We're getting closer," Khan called out.

"Good." Raven's smile was back.

"Why do you work for Silk Road?" Dani suddenly asked the woman. "How can all this be worth it?"

One dark eyebrow rose. "I get to travel the

world, put my unique talents to work, and make a lot of money doing it."

Dani's gut tightened. God, that sounded like Dani's life. Except, she wasn't a murdering psychopath.

"I'm not the white-picket-fence kind of woman." Raven's gaze dropped down Dani's body. "You don't seem to be, either. Traveling, doing as I please, suits me, and it allows me to avoid the messy entanglements that life always seems to thrust upon us."

"You mean connecting with another human being."

"You aren't married, are you, Ms. Navarro? No significant other, no dating, and from what my men showed me of your background, you aren't close to your family." Raven paused in front of Dani. "So, it seems you don't like messy entanglements, either. We really are alike."

"No." Yes, Dani realized she'd avoided relationships...but not because she didn't want them. Because she'd been afraid. Protecting herself.

She wasn't like this evil bitch. Cal had broken her open, and now, Dani wanted it all.

Suddenly, the trees disappeared. They stepped out on to the edge of the lake.

The others made startled exclamations. Dani took in the regular shape of the lake, the dark, still waters. It wasn't a natural lake. It was a baray.

Then she frowned. This hadn't been on the satellite maps they'd studied of the mountain. How could they have missed something like this?

"It is definitely man-made," Khan said. "Khmer construction representing the Sea of Creation." The man smiled. "This is the exact center of the quincunx."

"We're in the right place," Raven said. "Caspar, Daniels...into the water. I want to know what's down there."

The men dug around in one of the large packs they'd brought with them. They pulled out goggles and tiny air tanks.

Raven smiled smugly at Dani. "We're always prepared for anything."

Dani was pushed to her knees at the edge of the water, and she watched silently as the two men waded in. They ducked beneath the surface.

Time stretched on. Dani said a silent prayer that the men didn't find anything. She discreetly scanned the shoreline, hoping Cal was nearby. She had to be ready. He'd come for her.

There was a splashing sound and she jerked her attention back to the water. The men reappeared, heads above the water. Both of them were grinning.

"Raven, there's a temple. A huge-ass temple under the water on the bottom of this lake."

The woman nodded and grabbed herself a pair of goggles and a tank. "Casper, Daniels and Khan, you're with me." That steely-eyed gaze flicked toward Dani, and then to the man standing beside her. "Brock, you stay up here on lookout."

"And the woman?"

"We don't need her anymore." Raven settled the goggles over her face and stepped into the water. "Kill her."

All the air in Dani's chest turned hard. She watched the woman and her men disappear beneath the water. Dani's heart was a thundering pound in her ears.

She felt the man move behind her. His gun pressed to the base of her neck.

She closed her eyes, curling her hands into fists.

\*\*\*

Down on his belly, Cal crept closer. He could hear the quiet murmur of voices ahead.

Carefully, silently, he pushed a branch away. He saw the dark pool of water and took his time to count the number of Silk Road thugs. Four plus the leader.

He cursed under his breath. It was still bad odds when they had Dani right in the middle of them. He studied her as she watched the people sink into the water.

Chin lifted, her face a little pale but composed. She was hanging in there. *Just a bit longer, beautiful.*

He'd have to move around to a better vantage point and try to take a couple of them out quietly. He heard the sound of water and saw the two men had come back.

The red-headed leader sauntered forward, and a second later, the woman and three of her men disappeared into the dark-green water.

Cal grinned. That only left one. Then he frowned. Where the hell had he and Dani gone?

Cal moved again and then he saw her—and the man standing behind her with a gun pressed to her head.

Throat dry as dust, Cal surged to his feet. A red haze skimmed over his vision. *No.* Hell, no. *This is not happening again.* It was not happening to Dani.

He charged forward. He sprinted across the space, wishing for his gun.

But he was a former SEAL. Even his hands were deadly weapons.

The man heard him and spun. The gun fired.

Cal dived, rolled, heard the distinctive thump of bullets hitting the dirt. He leapt up and slammed into the man standing over Dani. As they went down, he saw Dani scrambling away. The man's fist crashed into Cal's jaw. With a grunt, he scissored his legs and punched back.

They traded more hard punches and then the man surged upward. He slammed Cal onto his back and all the air rushed out of Cal's lungs, pain exploding in his chest.

Suddenly, two more men that Cal hadn't seen earlier rushed out of the trees, shouting and lifting weapons.

No. *Dammit*, where the hell had they come from?

"Dani! Run," he bellowed.

Cal and his attacker rolled again. He saw the other two sprinting toward them. Cal blocked a hard punch, then countered with his own, driving his fist into the man's gut. With a cry, the man fell backward.

Cal jumped up and saw Dani hadn't run. She was on her hands and knees, trying to reach the guy's dropped weapon. She grabbed it and spun around.

The man Cal was fighting recovered, and his blow caught Cal in the side of his head. He tasted blood and arms wrapped around him, squeezing. Cal slammed the back of his head into the man's face. The man roared and blood sprayed over them.

A gunshot cracked through trees.

"Stop."

The deep, accented voice made Cal pause. He turned his head. Dani had been disarmed. The two reinforcements were standing near her, one with his weapon aimed at her chest, and the other with his aimed at Cal.

*Fuck. Fuck.* He dropped his arms to his sides. The man behind him released him and gave him a kick. He stepped in front of them, holding his broken nose.

"The boss wanted her dead." The guy's angry eyes settled on Cal. "I'm pretty sure she'd want you dead, too. He grabbed the gun from the other man and aimed it right between Cal's eyes.

Cal looked at Dani. Their eyes locked. Helpless rage roared inside him.

"I'm falling in love with you, Dani."

Her mouth dropped open.

The sudden, deafening boom of a shotgun made

Cal start. The man aiming at him fell backward with a groan, blood covering his chest.

Cal swiveled, bending into a protective crouch...to see Morgan Kincaid walking steadily out of the trees, holding a Benelli dual-mode shotgun.

There was more fire, and Cal turned again to see Logan O'Conner walking calmly out of the trees on the other side, firing a large Desert Eagle handgun.

Cal dived and tackled Dani out of the way. As they rolled through the dirt, he heard the sound of more gunfire. He held his body over Dani's. "Stay down. It'll be over soon."

When the gunfire stopped, Cal sat up. "Are you okay?" He cupped her cheek.

She gave a jerky nod. "I am now." She threw her arms around him. "God, I was so afraid they'd killed you."

"I got you, beautiful." He breathed her in. A shadow crossed over them and Cal looked up. "First time ever, I'm happy to see your scruffy face, O'Connor."

Logan grunted. "You're welcome."

Cal looked over and saw Morgan busy leaning down, tying up the Silk Road mercenaries. She yanked hard enough on the zip ties to make Cal wince.

"This it?" Morgan asked.

"Sorry it wasn't enough for you." He glanced back at Logan. "Damn glad you guys arrived when you did. Thanks."

"There are more under the water," Dani said.

"Including the woman in charge. Raven."

Her voice was a little shaky, but solid. Cal kept his arm wrapped tight around her. "Four in the water with short-range air tanks."

Dani's head dropped against his shoulder and he felt a shiver run through her. "I…I thought I was dead."

He pressed his lips against hers, pulling her closer. The taste of her flooded him, and she made a small sound, her hands clenching on him.

"You going to introduce us?" Logan said dryly. "Or just keep devouring the woman?"

Cal lifted his head. He'd completely forgotten about Logan and Morgan. "Dani, this degenerate is Logan O'Connor. For some unknown reason, my brother and I hired him for Treasure Hunter Security. The badass with the shotgun is Morgan Kincaid. She's very good to have on your side, and I suggest you don't go near her bad side. Guys, Daniela Navarro."

Dani smiled. "Hi, and it's Dani. Thanks for the rescue."

Logan lifted his chin.

Morgan nodded. "I have a photo of yours. A shot of Macchu Picchu with a layer of cloud resting on it. It's one of my favorites."

"You do?" Cal said, incredulous.

Morgan's face turned sour. "You don't have to sound so surprised, Ward. I like nice things."

"I thought you decorated with guns and knives."

"And the scalps of your victims," Logan added.

Morgan shifted her shotgun to rest against her

shoulder. "Both your scalps would look pretty good over my fireplace, now that you mention it."

Cal tightened his hold on Dani. "Never sure if she's joking when she says stuff like that."

Dani smiled at Morgan. "I love that Macchu Picchu shot as well. Sounds like you have excellent taste."

"Thank you."

Cal was just mildly shocked when he saw the tiniest smile tip Morgan's lips. He turned back to Dani and pulled her camera over his head. He held it out to her. "I think this belongs to you."

Her smile was blinding. "Thank you."

Logan shifted, staring at the pond. "Why are these bastards in the water?"

Dani let Cal help her to her feet. "A lost temple and a priceless artifact."

Logan shook his head. "Fucking Silk Road." Then he slapped a hand against his neck. "And fucking mosquitoes. I hate the jungle."

"You hate everything." Cal looked at the water. "They're armed. The leader is a woman, and she's meaner than you, Morgan."

Morgan raised a brow. "We'll see. I was just thinking I fancy a swim." Morgan slipped her backpack off her shoulders and reached in. She pulled out some small, sleek masks.

Cal's eyebrows rose. "You got your hands on Poseidon masks."

"Poseidon masks?" Dani said.

Morgan shot them that faint smile again. "Experimental dive masks. Sort of an artificial gill that'll extract oxygen from the water. They aren't on the market yet. I have a friend." She handed Cal a mask. "They don't work for long, so they're only good for short dives."

Dani craned her head. "What else do you have in there?"

"I'm ready for anything." Morgan patted the backpack. "We could climb a mountain, cross an ice floe, have a nice little candlelit dinner for two."

"You can sure as hell bet she's got more weapons in there," Logan grumbled.

Dani fiddled with the strap on her camera and pulled out what looked like a clear plastic bag. "Marine bag. Protects my camera from water."

Cal turned to Dani, gripping her shoulders. "I want you to stay here."

She bristled. "To hell with that, Cal. We've come this far, and I'm not giving up."

Morgan raised a brow. "Might be more dangerous for her to stay here. More of them could arrive."

Frustration rose up to choke Cal. "Fine. But you stay by my side." He held out a palm to Morgan. "Give me that little Condor knife you carry."

"Fine." Morgan pulled a small, sheathed knife from her boot and slapped it into his hand. "But you lose it, you buy me a new one."

Cal slipped it into Dani's pocket. "Just in case you need it."

She nodded. Then she expertly slipped her camera in the marine bag and sealed it. "I've used this a lot when I've crossed rivers or had to enter water on the job. Even has a glass piece that fits over the lens to take shots underwater. Works great."

"All right." Cal turned toward the water. "Let's go save the day."

Everyone pulled their Poseidon masks over their mouths. He checked the fit of Dani's mask, then led her into the water. It trickled in through his clothes. Cooler than he'd expected.

A moment later, the four of them stood waist deep, staring at the dark water. A feeling of deja vu washed over him. How many times had he stood like this, the familiar sensation of water lapping at him and his team by his side, before a SEAL mission?

But he'd never had the woman he was falling in love with by his side as he did it. Fear skittered down his spine. He'd keep her safe. Even if he died doing it.

He nodded at the others and sank beneath the surface.

# Chapter Twelve

It was far darker than she'd imagined.

Dani kicked through the water, holding on tight to Cal's hand and trying to match his powerful kicks. The deep-green water meant they couldn't see very far ahead of them. At first, she was sucking on her Poseidon mask too hard, and she slowly forced herself to relax. She'd done a bit of SCUBA diving in the past, and had always enjoyed it.

But this dark, murky water, and whatever ancient secrets it was hiding, was an entirely different thing.

She felt Cal's fingers tighten on hers, and her breathing eased.

Ahead, she could just make out Morgan and Logan kicking cleanly through the water. Logan had some sort of flashlight on, the beam barely making a dent in the murk.

They arrowed downward. God, how deep was this reservoir? She saw Logan pull up and make a hand signal. She strained to see... *There*. She could make out dark shadows looming ahead.

Dani's eyes widened. *Oh, my God.*

The temple rose up out of the gloom like some sort of dream. It was perfect. There was no rubble or tumbled towers. The water had kept it preserved, except for a coat of slime and the weeds growing up from the base of the baray.

It looked like a smaller version of Angkor Wat. Four towers in the corners and a larger tower in the center. Logan made another gesture and Cal nodded. They changed direction, heading toward a large arch that had to be the front entrance to the temple.

Dani kicked hard and followed Cal. She really hoped Raven and her goons weren't waiting for them.

They swam through the arch and into a wide, stone tunnel. Logan's flashlight was the only thing helping them see. It flashed over the smooth stone.

Then she saw something ahead. A set of stone stairs. She watched Logan and Morgan reach it. They pointed upward and rose.

Cal gripped Dani's hip and pushed her upward. A second later, her head broke the surface.

Cal stayed low in the water, pressing a finger to his mask warning her to be quiet. She nodded. With his wet hair slicked against his head and his mask on, he looked dark and dangerous.

Everyone pulled their masks off and clipped them to their belts. Cal traded hand signals with the others and they quietly went up the steps and out of the water.

At the top, she noted wet footprints on the stone.

Raven had definitely come this way.

There was another grand arch, leading into the main part of the temple. They moved forward cautiously, Cal and the others lifting their guns and tipping them to drain the water from the barrels.

Dani didn't know much about guns, but she guessed the small swim hadn't affected them.

The lower gallery they walked down was covered with beautiful engravings, reminiscent of the Angkor and the linga temple.

Dani pulled the plastic cover off her camera and took a few snaps. To see a place like this, undisturbed and looking as it must have looked when the people who built it had left, had excitement sparking in her belly.

They moved through the main part of the temple and at the far wall, she saw another archway. Logan shone his flashlight inside, and it illuminated a dank set of stairs leading down.

Dani focused on trying to move as quietly as the others. For big, deadly people, they sure moved with a light touch.

The staircase wrapped around in a spiral going down, down, down. She wondered how deep it went and marveled at the engineering it must have taken to build the place. Just how valuable was the cintamani stone to warrant a temple like this?

She took a deep breath. She guessed they had a good chance of finding the stone. Surely no one had ever discovered it here inside a sunken temple, beneath a mysterious lake in the middle of a remote jungle.

She just hoped they found it before Silk Road.

Ahead, Morgan stopped. She peered through a doorway, then nodded at the others.

They all stepped out into a huge underground cavern.

Dani pressed a hand to her mouth to control her gasp.

"Shit," Logan muttered.

"Never seen anything like this before," Morgan whispered, shaking her head.

Dani lifted her camera, but then lowered it. First, she just allowed herself to experience and admire the space.

It was an underground forest. There was light filtering in from somewhere. The slick stone walls were intersected with large veins of gems that glittered brightly. Parts of the walls were covered in some sort of fungus that glowed in multi-colored hues—bright yellow-green, blues, pinks and a dash of red and orange. She moved closer to the nearest tree. The leaves sparkled, made of a crystalline structure.

She lifted the camera and took shots of the trees and walls. The veins in the wall were mostly a deep green—jade, maybe jasper. Here and there, she spotted some large geometric clumps of brilliant white dotted on the wall. She stilled. Surely they couldn't be diamonds?

"It's just how they described the legend of Kunlun Mountain," Dani said. "Bejeweled plants and rock-like gems."

"Yeah. Doubt Silk Road will leave a place like

this undisturbed." Cal's gaze turned deadly. "Let's go find our *friends*."

They moved quietly through the sparkling trees. Dani promised herself she'd come back here and document this amazing place. Dr. Oakley and the team were going to be ecstatic.

"Where the hell are Silk Road?" Morgan murmured.

"Can't be far away," Cal answered. "Stay sharp."

They cleared the trees and Dani gasped. "Look."

There was a set of carved stone steps leading up to a platform covered with elegant arches. In the center of the platform was a stone pedestal.

And sitting on it was a large, pearl-gray stone.

"The cintamani," Dani said with awe.

"That's right," a cold voice replied. "And it's mine."

They all spun, Cal and the others raising their weapons.

Raven and her men had their guns aimed as well.

Dani's heart knocked against her ribs. *Standoff.*

\*\*\*

Cal kept his SIG pointed directly at the Silk Road woman.

"You two just won't die." Raven stared at Cal and then Dani. "The cintamani is mine. I might have to use it to make a wish that meddling Treasure Hunter Security members die a painful death."

"You don't really believe the stone is magical, do you?" Dani asked.

The woman raised one shoulder. "Hell, no. But others believe...and they will pay big bucks for it. Besides, it's an enormous pearl. Even without the ability to grant the owner's wildest dreams, it's worth a fortune."

Dani shook her head. "And you don't care who you hurt and kill in the process. You have no soul."

The woman gave a thin smile. "Short answer...no. My bosses are particular and unforgiving. But they pay well."

As the woman talked, Cal ran through all their options. It was three against four. He knew his guys could take the Silk Road thugs...but he couldn't risk Dani getting hurt in the chaos.

A flash of movement in the trees caught Cal's eyes. He heard a faint noise. Something sliding over rock.

He eyed the trees right behind Raven. Saw a flash of black. *What the hell?*

Raven stepped forward, her gun aimed at Dani's head. "I'm going to make sure this sticks this time."

"Screw you," Dani said.

"You shoot her, I'll shoot you."

"And my men will shoot you and your team."

Cal saw the movement in the trees again. Whatever the hell it was, he hoped he could use it to his advantage.

Suddenly, one of the Silk Road men screamed. A huge, black body struck from out of the trees.

With horror flooding his chest, Cal grabbed Dani

and yanked her backward.

The giant black snake slammed into Raven, knocking her off her feet.

"What—?" Raven's mouth formed an O.

The snake curled its massive body around the woman, lifting her off the ground. She struggled, crying out. Her gun fell from her fingers, clattering on the stone floor.

Frozen, Cal just stared at the snake. The damn thing was as thick around as Cal was and it had to be at least forty feet long.

"What the fuck is that?" Logan said.

"Naga," Dani breathed.

Black scales flashed, there was a crunch, and the woman's screams were abruptly cut off.

"Back up," Cal said quietly. "Very slowly."

The four of them backed up. The Silk Road men started firing at the creature. It reared up higher than all of them, and then, faster than Cal thought possible, it struck the closest one. The man fell, and then the snake went after the last Silk Road man.

"Keep moving," Cal said. How could they kill this thing?

The snake spun to face them. Cal felt Dani's hand tighten in his.

"Don't move," he whispered frantically.

"Fuck this." Morgan whipped her shotgun around.

Dani pressed into Cal's side. "If we die...well, I want you to know that I'm falling in love with you, too."

Heedless of the terror in front of them, he looked

down at her. Funny that he suspected those words were more terrifying for her than the giant snake. "Dani—"

"You don't have to say anything."

Something in his chest loosened. The way she was looking at him right now—with love in her eyes—made him realize he wanted to wake up to that face every day. He wanted to see her laugh, to watch her with her camera in hand, focused on her work, to see her flushed with pleasure, angry at him, to watch as he kissed her into forgiving whatever jackass mistake he was bound to make.

He realized that since he'd lost Marty and left the SEALs, he hadn't really been living. He'd been running from caring about anyone.

He yanked her closer. "I love you too, dammit."

"Knew you'd take the fall, Ward," Logan said smugly.

"Quiet," Morgan hissed. "Giant, killer snake, remember?" She tossed Cal a look. "You guys have terrible timing." Then she stiffened.

Cal looked back and saw the snake sliding their way.

"No one move," he breathed.

It came closer and Dani's fingers clenched on his hard enough to hurt. It slithered right past Cal, sliding against his leg. He closed his eyes and gritted his teeth. It was so fucking creepy.

The snake swept around again and rose up, making him think of a cobra, even though it didn't have a hood.

Its eerie green eyes seemed to look right through

them. He swore it was like it was…assessing them.

Cal tensed, ready to toss Dani behind him.

\*\*\*

Dani clutched Cal's hand and in her other, she gripped her camera tight.

Watching the giant snake right in front of them woke some primitive terror deep in her head. She was barely staying still, wanting to give into the primal urge to run.

She didn't want to die here. She wanted to live. Really live.

Cal loved her. No one had ever truly loved her before.

Suddenly, a gunshot broke the tense silence. One of the Silk Road men had sat up and shot at the snake.

The creature hissed and reared back. When it shot toward the man, Dani looked away. The screams echoed off the walls and a second later, stopped.

Then again, the sound of scales sliding on stone. She lifted her head and saw the snake was back, staring at them once more.

"Should I shoot it?" Morgan asked.

"No," Cal bit out.

Dani had to admit that, when she looked past her terror, the creature was elegant and near-beautiful. Inky-black scales, a powerful sinuous body, those stunning, jewel-like eyes.

"You are striking," she said.

The creature's gaze shifted to her.

Without thinking, she lifted her camera and pressed the button.

The flash seemed to startle the snake. It pulled back, and when she took another shot, it gave them one last look before slithering back into the trees.

Cal released a long breath and then pulled her in for a quick hug. "Nice work, Navarro."

"I just wanted a photo of it."

He gave a strangled laugh. "Of course you did."

She wrapped her arms around him and held on. "Can we just get the cintamani stone and get the hell out of here?"

"I second Dani's idea," Morgan said.

"I hate snakes," Logan growled.

Dani saw Cal roll his eyes. "Come on," he said. "Let's get the stone."

Still holding hands, they walked up the steps to the platform. Morgan and Logan stayed at the bottom, guns up, watching for any more visitors of the two—or no-legged—variety.

Dani and Cal paused in front of the pedestal. The mystical cintamani stone, sacred linga that had founded the Khmer Empire, was indeed a huge, oval-shaped black pearl. The light reflected flawlessly off its glossy surface. It was stunning.

They stood there for a second looking at it. "Go on," she said. "You do the honors."

Cal lifted the large pearl into his hands. She took a shot of the moment, loving the look on his face.

"So, does it work?" she asked.

He frowned at her. "What do you mean?"

She smiled. "Is it magic? Did it make your dreams come true?"

He reached out, and with that large, scarred hand, stroked her cheek. "I have no idea. My dreams came true a couple of minutes ago when you said you loved me."

God, apparently her man had a buried romantic streak. "I said I was *falling* in love."

He touched his mouth to hers. "You'll fall the rest of the way. Guaranteed."

"Cocky."

"Absolutely."

There was a loud sigh from below. "If you two can tear yourselves away from each other..." Morgan's amused voice. "I'll remind you again about the giant. Killer. Snake."

"How about we get out of here?" he said. "Go find ourselves a big bed. We'll order room service and not come out for a few days." He leaned in close and lowered his voice. "Bet I can make your dreams come true without you needing this stone."

"You're on, Ward. I do have this dream of photographing you nude."

He shook his head. "Not that dream."

"We'll see."

They descended the stairs and joined the others.

"We going now?" Morgan asked.

"Yep," Cal answered.

Logan slapped at his neck and cursed. "Good. I hate the jungle."

# Chapter Thirteen

Logan hacked through the jungle with his machete. Their trek away from the temple had proven uneventful so far.

An underwater temple protected by a big-ass snake. That had been a new one for him. He sliced some vines away. That was one thing about working for Treasure Hunter Security. You never knew what you were going to discover on a job.

He looked over at where Cal had a very secure arm around Dani Navarro. The two of them looked like they'd been through hell. But they were smiling at each other.

*Damn.* It didn't take a rocket scientist to see Callum Ward had taken the dive off the very high cliff called love. Logan shook his head. Before the mission, he'd ribbed Cal about finding a woman. Logan hadn't actually believed he would.

Well, it looked like Cal had finally found that someone who'd make him slow down. The Ward Clan would be thrilled.

Logan frowned. Except with Dec and Cal both paired off, the others might feel the need to turn their attention on him. Hmm, he might need to throw Hale under the bus and have Darcy and the others worry about finding Hale his perfect woman.

Logan was damn sure the perfect woman for him didn't exist. He'd thought he'd found her once and he couldn't have been more wrong.

He'd ended up with a woman more like that Raven bitch back at the temple. Now, he was more interested in his work and his friends. The occasional hookup was fine, but beyond that, he was steering well clear of women.

On his back, he felt the weight of the cintamani stone nestled in his backpack.

All this drama for a giant pearl. Fucking Silk Road was turning into a dangerous pain in the ass. Logan scowled at the trees. God only knew what they had planned next, but he needed to talk to Dec. They needed to discuss what they could do to help Agent Burke bring the fuckers down.

He reached up and checked the backpack, feeling the outline of the stone through the canvas.

Damn stone was supposed to make your wishes come true.

If that were true, maybe he would wish for his perfect woman... Logan snorted. *Yeah, right.*

From his left, Morgan called out. "Come on, O'Connor, you're slacking. If you swing like that, we won't make it back to civilization before I'm fifty."

"Quit your bitching, Kincaid."

Sweat dripped down his face. For now, maybe he'd just wish that his next job was not in the damn jungle.

\*\*\*

Dani stood back and watched Cal hand the cintamani stone to Dr. Oakley.

They were in the private room off the restaurant back at the Heritage Hotel in Siem Reap, where she'd photographed Cal planning their expedition.

God, it was only days ago, but it felt like months. Back then, she'd taken an instant dislike to Cal, pigeon-holing him to protect herself.

Well, it had only taken a wild, dangerous jungle treasure hunt to break down her walls and have her fall in love with him.

She lifted her camera and took the shot. Cal's grin. Dr. Oakley's amazement and awe. The rest of the team—minus Jean-Luc—stood nearby. They still looked a little battered around the edges but they were smiling.

The others had made it back to the bikes, and their local guides had gotten them back to Siem Reap and rushed Jean-Luc to the hospital.

Cal and Dani had made it out of the jungle with Logan and Morgan. Cal had gone to deal with Oakley and the others and check in with the Treasure Hunter Security office. Dani had managed a shower and to find some food before she'd collapsed in her bed. Cal had crawled in sometime during the night and held her as they'd slept. They hadn't had much of a chance to talk this morning, since they had to meet Dr. Oakley and the others.

"Jean-Luc will love it," Dr. Oakley said, worry

etched on his face.

The French archeologist's gunshot wound had gotten infected. He was fighting for his life in the hospital.

She watched Cal's face change, harden. She took a step closer and pressed a hand to his shoulder.

Cal cleared his throat. "I'm sorry I couldn't stop him from getting hurt—"

Dr. Oakley shook his head. "You did more than any man can be expected to do. I'm so grateful you were with us, Cal. I suspect more of us would be hurt or dead if you hadn't been. No one is to blame for Jean-Luc's injuries but the Silk Road."

"He's tough," Gemma added. "Maybe we should threaten not to let him see the cintamani until he gets better."

The others laughed.

Cal gave a short nod. "You'll see the stone gets put somewhere safe? Where it can be appreciated and safeguarded?"

Dani knew exactly who it needed to be safeguarded from.

"I've already been making plans with the Cambodian government." A wide smile crossed Dr. Oakley's face. "They're organizing a special exhibit and extra security."

Sakada stirred. "And we have new funding. We're going to head back to Phnom Kulen to study the Cintamani Temple where you found the stone."

"Ah…you remember the snake, right?" Cal said.

"The really big snake," Dani added. "We weren't exaggerating."

"Yes," Dr. Oakley said. "I've always suspected legends and myths had a seed of truth. I guess we know that's definitely true of the naga legends." The older man's gaze moved to Cal. "We want Treasure Hunter Security to come with us. I want to ensure everyone on this team stays safe."

"That can be arranged," Cal answered.

Dr. Oakley's attention moved to Dani. "Dani, we'd love to have you, too."

"Well—"

Cal stood and tugged her closer. "Not for a while, doc. We have a trip planned."

She looked up at him. "We do?"

"Yes. And it doesn't involve any jungles."

There were chuckles from the others.

"Were you planning to ask me?"

"Nope."

She pulled back, her hands on her hips. "I might be in love with you, Cal Ward, but that doesn't mean you get to pull your alpha male, I'm-in-charge stupidity—"

He grabbed her and tossed her over his shoulder.

"Cal!"

She heard the others laughing now, and for a moment, it stemmed her anger. It was a good sound.

But Cal didn't need the encouragement.

She wriggled against him, and hammered her hands on his back. He strode down the hall, and seconds later, they were in her room.

He set her down and the next thing she knew he

was cupping her face. The serious look on his face made her swallow her teasing comments.

"Since I lost my friend Marty—" emotion clogged Cal's voice "—I vowed to live for him. Climbing, parasailing, surfing, skydiving...you name it, I did it. The faster and more dangerous, the better." He tucked a strand of her hair behind her ear. "And women."

Pithy words came to her, but she stayed quiet.

He stroked her cheeks. "But what I feel for you made me realize that I wasn't living. I was using my promise as an excuse to keep moving, keep leaping, keep running and not let anyone too close."

She understood. God, she understood better than anyone. "I've done the same, Cal. Let my work and travel stop me from connecting. From risking my heart."

Cal nodded. "In that underwater temple...I realized that apart from my family, everything else in my life was gloss, no substance."

Her breath hitched. "And now?"

His lips moved just a whisper from hers. "I want to live, beautiful. Want to make a life with me?"

Joy flooded her. "I'm game."

With a laugh, he scooped her into his arms and then dumped her on the bed. His hands went to his shirt, opening the buttons.

"Now...I seem to recall promising you naughty, dirty things."

***

Cal woke up slowly, stretching in his bed. His empty bed. He reached over and patted the sheets beside him. They were cool but there was a faint impression left in the pillow.

With a lazy smile, he pulled on his jeans and headed for the kitchen of his mountain cabin. As he made himself a coffee, he stared out the window. The sun was rising, casting a golden glow over the mountains. He heard his cell phone beep, and absently snatched it off the bench. When he read the text, he rolled his eyes. He was surprised he'd held them off this long.

Coffee in hand, he headed out onto the deck. The morning air was cool on his bare chest. Cal leaned against the railing and sipped his coffee. He didn't think anywhere was quite as beautiful as the Rocky Mountains.

Before, when he'd come up here, he was usually too busy planning a climb or a bike ride to sit here and soak in the view.

But now...he took a deep breath and watched the golden light deepen and the day begin. "To you, buddy." Cal lifted his coffee mug, and hoped that wherever Marty was now that he was happy.

The brighter light let him spot the slim figure moving down the hill. She was crouched, her camera in hand, capturing the view.

He descended the steps and made his way down to her. They'd been back from Cambodia a few weeks, and they'd spent the time alone, just the two of them, indulging in whatever the hell they wanted. Heaven.

She sensed him coming and turned, her wide smile warming something deep inside him. When he reached her, he pulled her close, kissing the side of her neck, before moving on to her delicious lips. "Morning. Beautiful out here today." He watched as the sun gilded her skin, turning it golden.

"Yeah, it is." She reached over and nabbed his coffee, taking a long sip. "I wanted to catch some pre-sunrise shots, but I just sat here, absorbing it all, and missed the chance."

She didn't seem worried about it.

"Are you planning to go climbing today?" she asked.

Cal had no desire to climb anything. He stole his coffee back. "Nope." He nuzzled into her neck. "I can think of some other things we can do. Together." He was far more interested in making moments with Dani. Giving her pleasure, watching her open herself more and more to him.

"Really?" She turned toward him. "Like what?"

"Like me showing you, in every way possible, how much I love you." He rubbed his nose against hers. "One kiss. One caress. One naughty moment at a time."

He saw her breath hitch in her chest. "I like the way you think."

He took her hand, and they started back up toward the cabin.

"I've got lots of ideas." Then he screwed up his nose. "Damn. I forgot. My mother just sent a message. The Ward family are descending on us for lunch, whether we like it or not. That probably means Logan, Morgan and whoever isn't out on a mission will also come. They'll be here in a few hours."

She smiled. "I can't wait to meet everyone."

He made a rude sound. "My mother, well, she's bossy, opinionated—"

"I've met her once, Cal. She's amazing. And you love her, so I'll love her."

His mom was going to go crazy over Dani. Cal knew his mother was just giddy that her son had taken the plunge.

"So," Dani dragged the word out. "Let's just see what you can do with a couple of hours, Ward."

Desire slammed into him. "That a challenge?"

She pulled them to a stop, her hands sliding into the waistband of his jeans, her fingers tickling his abs. "Can I take some shots of you? Without these on?"

"No." He turned her and pushed her in the direction of the cabin.

"Come on—"

"No."

"I'm not going to show anybody."

"No." He swung her into his arms, enjoying the sound of her laughter. "But whatever else you want to do to my naked body...well, I'm all yours."

Her eyes softened. "Always?"

"Always."

---

I hope you enjoyed Callum and Dani's story!

Treasure Hunter Security continues with *Unexplored*, the story of former Navy SEAL Logan O'Connor and classy, elegant CEO Sydney Granger on a dangerous adventure into the Andean cloud forests. Read on for a preview of the first chapter.

**Don't miss out!** For updates about new releases, action romance info, free books, and other fun stuff, sign up for my VIP mailing list and get your *free box set* containing three action-packed romances.

Visit here to get started:
www.annahackettbooks.com

FREE BOX SET DOWNLOAD

**JOIN THE ACTION-PACKED ADVENTURE!**

Formats: Kindle, ePub, PDF

# Preview: Unexplored

Thank God her crappy day was almost over.

Sydney Granger walked into her office, wanting nothing more than to kick off her high heels. Her aching feet were killing her. She sighed. But she still had work to do before she could head back to her condo and relax with a glass of wine.

She sank down in the black-leather office chair behind her sleek, glossy desk. The meeting with the board had...not gone well. She touched her aching temple. It had been two months since she'd taken over as CEO of Granger Industries, and the board members were still nervous. All they saw was a wealthy heiress who was inexperienced in business, real estate, and construction.

Sydney shrugged to herself. She was used to people underestimating her.

She swiveled in her chair and, for a second, stared out at the glowing lights of Washington, D.C. She had an excellent view of the grand dome of the Capitol Building. She knew D.C.—had been born and raised here—but she was still finding her feet in the new job. And behind closed doors, she secretly wondered if she'd ever get there.

Glancing back at her desk, she saw the files stacked neatly on the corner by her executive assistant. Then she looked at her laptop. Sydney knew if she opened it, she'd have a ton of emails to deal with. That glass of wine had never seemed further away.

What the hell...there was no one left in the office at this time of night, so she released the clip in her hair. No one to see the new CEO kicking back. The pale-gold strands fell down to brush her shoulders.

Her gaze fell on the framed photo resting on the corner of her desk. It was a picture of her with her father and brother. It had been taken a few years ago, and they were all grinning for the camera. *Why the hell did you leave me the company, Dad?* Still reeling from her father's sudden death, she'd been stunned when he'd left the lion's share of the company to her. Her brother, Drew, had inherited stock in the company as well. Drew had a sky-high IQ, and probably knew way more about the business and the company. But she knew that for all his brilliance, her socially awkward brother wasn't a businessman.

For some reason, her father had wanted *her* to be CEO of Granger.

God, she missed him. Since her mother had died when Sydney was ten, it had just been the three of them. Grief and guilt were a gnawing hollow ache inside her. But Sydney didn't let it show. She'd been raised in Washington society, and she was damn good at hiding her feelings. At the glittering gatherings, so many people were just waiting for the slightest show of emotion to pounce and spread the gossip. She remembered the insincere faces and condescending pats after her mother had died.

Sydney leaned back in her chair. The CIA should just send their agents to train at society parties and gallery openings. Then they'd have the best poker faces around. She touched the frame. Had it really been two months since her father had died in that explosion? Terrorists had been targeting a foreign diplomat who'd been staying at the same hotel, and her father had been caught in the blast.

"I'm so sorry, Dad."

Now, Sydney was here, buried in her work at Granger Industries. Drew, unable to cope, had run off to South America. His latest interest was in history and archeology. The guy had a collection of degrees—she sighed—but he never stuck with one thing. Last month, he'd been talking about launching an online tech company. Next month, who knew? He'd probably take up race car driving.

Sydney rubbed her temple again. She had reports to read, forms to sign, tomorrow's meetings to prepare for. She was trying, but right now, she just felt like she was drowning. Most days she was barely managing to keep her head above water.

It had to get better, but there was a little voice in the back of her head whispering with a whole lot of glee that she'd fail. Again. It loved to remind her that she'd screwed up her last job…and that others had paid the price. She glanced over at the photo of her father again, and her throat tightened.

The ringing of the phone on her desk startled her. She frowned. It was late. Who'd be calling at this time?

She snatched up the receiver. "Sydney Granger."

"Ms. Granger, listen and do not talk."

The electronically-altered voice made her stiffen. "Who is this—?"

"Quiet. Your brother's life depends on it."

Sydney's hand clenched on the phone. "This is about Drew?"

"We have your brother in Peru. If you want him back alive, you come to Lima and be prepared to transfer five million dollars to us to secure his freedom. We will contact you again then."

*What?* Her heart started to pound. *Stay calm, Sydney. Keep them talking. Get as much information as you can.* "How do I know this isn't a hoax?" She looked blindly out the window, the lights of the city now just a blur. "I want to talk with him—"

"I make the demands, not you. My only proof...I am Silk Road."

The line went dead.

Sydney set the phone back down with a shaky hand. Silk Road? Who the hell was Silk Road?

She'd spoken to Drew a few days ago. He'd been fine. Excited. He was on the trail of an ancient pre-Incan culture. He'd been visiting museums, meeting with local archeologists, and talking about heading into the Andes. He'd been yammering on about the ruins he planned to visit, and talking about all the research he'd been doing.

But for all his amazing intelligence, her brother was a bit oblivious to regular life. It would be so easy to snatch him.

*God.* If these people hurt him... Drew was all Sydney had left.

She forced herself to breathe. *Think, Sydney.* Did this have something to do with her previous employment? Her former role had been highly classified. None of her friends or family had known about the work she'd done. To the world, she'd been a Washington socialite who cared mostly about designer clothes, fancy parties, and museum openings.

She quickly opened her laptop and logged on. She typed in a search on Silk Road.

A few minutes later, she sat back in her chair, dread settling in her belly. There wasn't much, but what she'd learned wasn't good. Silk Road appeared to be a dangerous, black-market antiquities syndicate. Not much was known about them, except that they were well-funded, well-connected, and ruthless.

Something else caught her attention. Over the last few months, the group had tangled with a private security firm that specialized in security for archeological digs, expeditions, and museum exhibits. Treasure Hunter Security. She tilted her head at the fun name. It appeared that this firm had beaten Silk Road—twice.

She typed in another search, and pulled up the website for Treasure Hunter Security.

They were based in Denver but worked all across the world. She scrolled through the pages and stopped at an image showing three men—all of them wearing khaki clothes and holsters—standing shoulder-to-shoulder. Declan and Callum Ward were the owners of the company. Former Navy SEALs, and from the look of them, tough and capable. Her gaze fell on the third man standing with them. He was slightly taller and a little broader than the Ward brothers. Big, with shaggy, long, brown hair and a rugged face. He looked like a man you didn't want to mess with.

Her gaze drifted back to the photograph on her desk and locked onto her brother's smiling face. Her stomach turned over.

She had to rescue Drew. And she needed Treasure Hunter Security to help her do it.

\*\*\*

Logan O'Connor stretched out, put his boots up on the arm of the couch and pulled his ball cap over his eyes.

Damn, he was tired.

After he'd returned from a job in the Cambodian jungle a month back—having rescued Callum's ass—he'd plunged straight into another job in the Gobi Desert. It'd been grueling, and hot, and sandy. He hated sand.

"Hey, boots off the couch!" A hand slapped at his boots.

Logan just growled.

His hat was whipped away. Darcy Ward stood there, glaring at him. As usual, she was all glossy and put-together. Not a single strand of her chin-length black hair was out of place and her blue-gray eyes were narrowed on him.

She tried to shift his boots again, but he kept them where they were.

"We have a client coming in, Logan," she said with a huff.

Logan grunted.

She pushed and shoved again, and finally his feet slid off to the polished concrete floor.

He sat up. "I'm damn glad I never had a sister."

She pulled a face at him.

"Go bother your *actual* brothers," he growled.

"They aren't here." Her nose screwed up. "Declan and Layne are upstairs. They should be down soon."

Dec—Logan's best friend—lived in the apartment above the Treasure Hunter Security offices.

Logan snorted. "I bet I know what the hell they're doing." Since his best friend had tumbled head-over-his-ass in love with Dr. Layne Rush, the man couldn't seem to stay away from his fiancée. "Those two are like fucking rabbits."

"No swearing in the office," Darcy snapped.

"Why?"

"We have a client coming in," she said with exaggerated patience. "She's flying in from D.C. She's the CEO of Granger Industries. This is going to be a good-paying job, Logan. Don't screw anything up."

Granger Industries? Logan had a vague recollection of real estate, or construction, or something. Just to piss Darcy off, Logan put his boots up on the coffee table. "Where's Cal?"

"On a trip with Dani. She's photographing the ruined city of Great Zimbabwe and Cal went with her."

Another man who couldn't stay away from his woman. Logan still couldn't believe his friends had gone and fallen in love. Dec and Cal—two of the toughest guys he'd ever known.

He heard footsteps, and since he hadn't heard the front door, he knew it was Dec. Actually, after years together on the SEAL teams, and now working together at THS, Logan could pick out Dec's footsteps anywhere.

"Darce. Logan." Declan crossed the large, open space of the converted warehouse.

Logan glanced at his friend. Dec was tall, muscled, with piercing gray eyes. He still looked the same as he always had, but these days, he seemed different. More relaxed, more at ease.

"Who's our new client?" Dec asked.

"Sydney Granger of Granger Industries." Darcy looked at her watch. "Her plane should've landed about an hour ago. She should be here soon."

Dec nodded and headed toward the small kitchenette in the corner of the space. He opened the fridge and pulled out a soda.

"Diet Coke?" Logan raised a brow.

"Layne is addicted to the stuff." Dec shrugged. "I've developed a taste for it."

Logan shook his head. "Next thing you'll tell me is that you want to do lunch, or go out for a damned manicure."

Dec's gray gaze narrowed. "No, but I'm thinking about kicking your ass."

Logan snorted. "You can try."

"Shush," Darcy said. "She's here. Try to look professional." She knocked Logan's boots off the coffee table.

Logan followed Darcy's gaze to the wall of flat screens at the end of the warehouse. That was Darcy's domain. She might look like she'd stepped out of a magazine, but the woman was a genius with computers. On the far screen, he saw security footage from the outside of the office. He saw what looked like a rental car parked near his truck, and caught a glimpse of blonde hair as a woman walked toward the front door of the warehouse.

The next thing he heard was the click of heels on concrete. Logan turned his head. And then he straightened.

The woman was tall, slender, and wearing a navy blue skirt that slicked over her gentle curves and a crisp white shirt. Blonde hair the color of champagne was caught back in some sort of complicated twist at the back of her head, accenting a face that was downright beautiful. She had a slim nose, perfectly formed lips, and high cheekbones. Pale-blue eyes skated over the room.

The woman had money and class written all over her.

Logan shifted on the couch. She was *so* not his type.

"Hi, Ms. Granger." Darcy stepped forward and held out her hand. "I'm Darcy Ward. This is my brother Declan."

"Thank you for seeing me. And please, call me Sydney." She shook hands with Darcy and then with Declan.

"Nice to meet you," Dec said.

"And this is one of our top security specialists, Logan O'Connor." Darcy gestured at Logan.

Logan didn't bother standing, just lifted his chin.

Sydney Granger gave him a cool stare before her gaze moved back to Declan and Darcy.

Yeah, he'd been dismissed by the Ice Queen. He was surprised he didn't have freezer burn.

"I need your help," Sydney said. "My brother needs your help."

Darcy gestured to the conference table off to the side. "Why don't you sit down? You wouldn't give us any details over the phone—"

Sydney Granger nodded. "I wasn't sure if it was safe." She sank into a chair. "My brother left for Peru several weeks ago. He has a history degree, and he wanted to explore an ancient culture down there—"

"Inca?" Dec asked.

"No. Have you ever heard of the Warriors of the Clouds? They're also called the Chachapoyas."

Logan frowned, and watched Darcy and Dec

shake their heads. Darcy reached over to tap on one of her keyboards, clearly planning to do a search.

"I hadn't either," Sydney answered. "But I did some research on the flight out here."

"They're from *Raiders of the Lost Ark*," Logan said.

Pretty blue eyes blinked at him. "Yes."

*Yeah, I'm not just a big, dumb idiot.* Logan was used to people taking one look at him and deciding he was big and dangerous but not very smart.

"The gold idol that Indy's after in the beginning of the movie—" he looked at the others "—you know, when he's escaping from the big, rolling boulder. That belonged to these warriors."

"That's right," Sydney Granger said in her cool, cultured voice. "But the movie isn't factual. The Chachapoyas weren't metalworkers, so they didn't have any golden idols. But they built cities and fortresses high in the cloud forests of the Andes. My brother estimated that only a small portion of their sites have been found so far. The Cloud Warriors fought off the Inca for years, and even helped the Spanish fight against the Inca. They were famed for being beautiful, and many of them were fair-skinned with pale-colored hair and eyes. Several of their mummies have been discovered, and some do have pale hair, and several descendants of the Chachapoyas today still have blonde hair, and blue or green eyes."

"Were they not native to the region?" Darcy asked. "Perhaps they came from somewhere else?"

Sydney tilted her head. "There are lots of theories. That they had come from Europe prior to the Spanish, that they were descended from the white, bearded god, Viracocha. Recent DNA testing shows they are from the Andes, indistinguishable from the others living in the area. They are from the cloud forests."

"What happened to the Cloud Warriors?" Logan asked.

"They held out, but eventually the Inca conquered them. They were forced to leave their cities, and then disease brought by the Spanish wiped them out."

"Okay, so what do these Warriors of the Clouds have to do with your brother?" Dec asked.

Logan watched the woman as she lifted her chin. Staring at her face, all he saw was icy perfection. No emotion, no distress, nothing. Yeah, she was a real cool one.

"I got a call at my office last night. A group says it has my brother and they want five million dollars in ransom. They said I have to go to Lima, Peru to carry out the transaction."

Logan shook his head to himself. Forget cool, she was ice all the way. Man, the woman didn't even look like her pulse jumped when she talked about her brother being held hostage. Ice water in those veins.

Dec was frowning. "We don't do a lot of ransom demands. We have interceded when some archeologists have been snatched off digs—"

Interestingly, Logan saw Sydney press her hands together on the table. Her fingers flexed, then relaxed. "I came to you because the group who have Drew...they call themselves Silk Road."

Now, Logan pushed to his feet. *Aw, hell.*

**Treasure Hunter Security**
Undiscovered
Uncharted
Unexplored

# MORE ACTION ROMANCE?

**ACTION
ADVENTURE
TREASURE HUNTS
SEXY SCI-FI ROMANCE**

When astro-archeologist and museum curator Dr. Lexa Carter discovers a secret map to a lost old Earth treasure—a priceless Fabergé egg—she's excited at the prospect of a treasure hunt to the dangerous desert planet of Zerzura. What she's not so happy about is being saddled with a bodyguard—the museum's mysterious new head of security, Damon Malik.

After many dangerous years as a galactic spy, Damon Malik just wanted a quiet job where no one tried to kill him. Instead of easy work in a museum full of artifacts, he finds himself on a backwater planet babysitting the most infuriating woman he's ever met.

She thinks he's arrogant. He thinks she's a trouble-magnet. But among the desert sands and ruins, adventure led by a young, brash treasure hunter named Dathan Phoenix, takes a deadly turn. As it becomes clear that someone doesn't want them to find the treasure, Lexa and Damon will have to trust each other just to survive.

**The Phoenix Adventures**
Among Galactic Ruins
At Star's End
In the Devil's Nebula
On a Rogue Planet
Beneath a Trojan Moon
Beyond Galaxy's Edge
On a Cyborg Planet
Return to Dark Earth
On a Barbarian World
Lost in Barbarian Space

# Also by Anna Hackett

**Treasure Hunter Security**
Undiscovered
Uncharted
Unexplored

**Hell Squad**
Marcus
Cruz
Gabe
Reed
Roth
Noah
Shaw
Holmes

**The Anomaly Series**
Time Thief
Mind Raider
Soul Stealer
Salvation
Anomaly Series Box Set

**The Phoenix Adventures**
Among Galactic Ruins
At Star's End
In the Devil's Nebula
On a Rogue Planet

Beneath a Trojan Moon
Beyond Galaxy's Edge
On a Cyborg Planet
Return to Dark Earth
On a Barbarian World
Lost in Barbarian Space

**Perma Series**
Winter Fusion

**The WindKeepers Series**
Wind Kissed, Fire Bound
Taken by the South Wind
Tempting the West Wind
Defying the North Wind
Claiming the East Wind

**Standalone Titles**
Savage Dragon
Hunter's Surrender
One Night with the Wolf

**Anthologies**
A Galactic Holiday
Moonlight (UK only)
Vampire Hunter (UK only)
Awakening the Dragon (UK Only)

For more information visit AnnaHackettBooks.com

# About the Author

I'm a USA Today bestselling author and I'm passionate about *action romance*. I love stories that combine the thrill of falling in love with the excitement of action, danger and adventure. I'm a sucker for that moment when the team is walking in slow motion, shoulder-to-shoulder heading off into battle.

I write about people overcoming unbeatable odds and achieving seemingly impossible goals. I like to believe it's possible for all of us to do the same.

My books are mixture of action, adventure and sexy romance and they're recommended for anyone who enjoys fast-paced stories where the boy wins the girl at the end (or sometimes the girl wins the boy!) For release dates, action romance info, free books, and other fun stuff, sign up for the latest news here:

Website: AnnaHackettBooks.com

Printed in Great Britain
by Amazon